Allosaurus in Wonderland and Other Tales of Avalonia

Jennifer Lee Rossman

Allosaurus in Wonderland and Other Tales of Avalonia

Published by
Agita Publishing (formerly From Beyond Press) | Chicago, IL
agitapublishing.com
mike@agitapublishing.com
Instagram & Bluesky: @agitapublishing

ISBN: 979-8-9925941-0-2
Library of Congress Control Number: 2025950717

Contents

To the storytellers
and the characters
and everyone in between

Allosaurus in Wonderland

'Twas brillig the morning I fell through the wormhole.

I got that word from a poem my father read to me once, brillig. I didn't know what it meant. Maybe nothing, or maybe it meant something different for everyone.

I just knew 'twas brillig that morning, the sky still sleepily wiping away the last wisps of a pink sunrise and the leaves wet with dew when I pushed them out of the way in my pursuit of . . .

To be honest, I'm still trying to figure out exactly what it was. Some sort of small, grayish-white mammal, capable of bipedal locomotion. Argyrolagus maybe, or leptictidium.

I was six. I thought it was a rabbit.

Whatever it was, I chased it through my backyard and into a wormhole. Not a big one, like the kind you see in movies, that you can fly an entire spaceship through. Just a small, little-girl-sized tear in the fabric of reality.

We don't like to think of the fabric of reality as being flimsy and easily torn. We don't like to think of it at all, just let it exist in the background without a second thought until something goes horribly wrong with it, like gallbladders or the government.

But it's there, space and time and dimensions we weren't built to understand, all woven together in a cosmic tapestry. It's the old newspaper crumpled up between snowglobes in a moving box marked "fragile," keeping our universe safe.

Only the truth is, the old newspaper might have more structural integrity, because sometimes the universe bumps into another. Sometimes hard enough to crack.

'Twas brillig on the other side of the wormhole, too, and for a minute I didn't notice that I had been transported to another world. I just kept chasing after that not-quite-rabbit, even after I lost sight of it as the bushes and undergrowth got thicker, even as I wandered farther than our property had ever extended before.

It was in the back of my head, the distant thought that I should have reached the neighbors' fence by now, but I ignored it. Maybe, if I didn't acknowledge something impossible was happening, maybe it would keep happening. Like the coyote in those cartoons who could walk on thin air so long as he didn't realize he was breaking the laws of physics.

The roar stopped me in my tracks.

It was a feeling more than a sound, this low, rumbling scream that vibrated in the air and in my chest. A growling tiger mixed with a train running at me full speed.

I had never heard anything like it. Never wanted to hear anything like it again. Neon warning lights flashed in my head and I scrambled to hide under a bush, trying to make myself as small as possible.

These were not our bushes. Our bushes had blackberries. I tried to ignore the lack of blackberries.

Curious, I peeked out after several long moments passed without another roar.

Those were not our trees. Some of them looked familiar, pine trees and maple trees and those ones with the white bark, but most of them looked completely alien, with a crown of leaves sitting atop scaly trunks with no branches.

Something from the cycadeoidaceae family, I know now, but back then I just knew they were dinosaur trees, like you would get in a cheap playset of scientifically inaccurate toys. Sets of three long claw marks in the bark confirmed it:

I was in another world, and it had dinosaurs.

I think I was exactly the right age for this. Old enough to understand my situation was impossible, but young enough to believe otherwise.

The rest of the forest made itself small too after it heard the roar, and we waited together, small and silent. Then slowly, bit by bit, we got big again.

Little birds and creatures I didn't quite recognize peeked up and announced the tentative safety to the rest, then some deer ventured out of their hiding places, moving as a herd with some plant-eating dinosaurs. With a crash of foliage, a creature the size of a car, not a turtle but bearing a striking resemblance, ambled on to wherever he had been going before the interruption.

I was the last to get big again, letting myself properly take in the world around me before joining it.

Nothing made sense here. Glyptodons—the mock turtles which I didn't know the name of but recognized from a book—didn't live at the same time as those magnificent brown and green mottled hadrosaurs. Millions of years separated them. Chickadees like we had at home flitted between branches, the silhouette of a pterodactyl flew overhead, and none of it made sense.

"Curious," I said to myself, and the forest got still again. Just for a second, like maybe a human who could talk was just as curious to these creatures as they were to me.

I wondered if all of them, or their ancestors, had run off after a strange rabbit like I did and ended up here in this world beyond our world. Maybe the dinosaurs escaped extinction here, or maybe this was a place where all the times connected and we had all just arrived.

I wondered if they could go back home, if I could, and in an instant all my wonder and curiosity stopped mattering. I turned and ran back the way I came.

Until that moment, I never thought of home as something I could lose, something that could go away or be lost. Home was a constant, it was forever, and no matter how long I went away, it was supposed to be there waiting when I got back.

It wasn't supposed to be fragile.

I ran on pure instinct, hoping my brain remembered the way home, hoping if I just ran far enough, the unfamiliar foliage would turn familiar and I would be back in my own yard.

Between the sound of my panicked breathing and my frantic crashing through the leaves, I didn't hear the dinosaur until it was almost too late.

She stood in a small clearing just large enough for her to turn around in comfortably, pacing back and forth in front of something shimmery hanging in the air. Her mouth was open slightly as she investigated, revealing impossibly large and sharp teeth, and as she pawed at the strange sparkling, I saw claws on her front limbs that looked as if they were designed specifically to snatch up little creatures like me.

Allosaurus, I decided in the brief moment before I remembered to be scared. Like a tyrannosaurus, but those didn't have those little ridges above their eyes.

And she was beautiful. Sort of a burnt red with darker stripes that reminded me of my grandma's brindle boxer dog, every part of her made of pure muscle and strength.

Maybe I made a noise, maybe she smelled me. I don't know. But her head swiveled suddenly, staring straight at me.

She took a step closer, and another, and I remembered to be scared now. Terrified, actually, as she looked down at me curiously with a tilt of her head that was longer than my entire body.

If she wanted to, she could gobble me up in one bite and my parents would never know what happened to me. I felt very small, and wished I could get even smaller.

The allosaurus leaned down, her face just feet from mine, sniffing and snuffling loudly. Her hot breath smelled like death.

I didn't dare move, I didn't dare breathe, but I felt tears slipping down my cheeks.

But she didn't eat me. Maybe she was still deciding if I looked tasty. Maybe she was marveling at me, this new and confusing creature like nothing she'd ever seen before.

Maybe she would let me go because I was cute and harmless.

I couldn't take that chance.

My feet were moving before the courage reached my brain, running at full speed, diving between the dinosaur's massive legs. And into that sparkling doorway I must not have seen in my pursuit of the not-quite-rabbit.

And there was my yard, no dinosaurs or anything, just familiar foliage and my house waiting for me. Just like I had never left.

The allosaurus roared, but it sounded far away, almost like a half-remembered dream, and then stopped suddenly. I turned, and the sparkling doorway between worlds was gone, my racing heart the only proof it had ever existed.

I decided not to tell anyone. They wouldn't believe me anyway.

But there was another world, just next to ours and somewhere beyond time, and 'twas brillig. I think I was the first human to step foot in that world.

I would not be the last.

Baryonyx and Clyde

They couldn't keep this up forever. Luck had been with them thus far—and it *was* luck, no matter how much Campbell boasted about his skills—but they kept pushing that luck, pushing it to the limit and then just a little farther, and Lindy knew it had to run out eventually.

They would be caught. Or trapped on the wrong side of a portal. Or eaten.

Lindy crossed her fingers, and kissed them for good measure, hoping that they wouldn't be eaten.

"Hey, focus," Campbell said softly as he continued filling his bag with brand new antiques, and gestured for her to do the same.

The 1930s may not have had security cameras, but Lindy still instinctively checked that her hoodie covered her distinctively turquoise hair before helping him loot the store. "We've been here too long," she pointed out.

In the dim glow of the gas streetlights from the front window, Lindy saw Campbell's dismissive wave. "We have time," he said, playfully twirling the dial of a rotary phone as he contemplated the future value it would have in mint condition.

They did, indeed, have time. In that, Campbell was absolutely correct. How much time, there was the rub, and Lindy was quite certain she used that phrase correctly. She had never been much for classic literature.

The portals—if there was a more technical term for them, she didn't know it—seemed to operate on their own schedule. Some would stay open for hours, others mere moments.

Lindy and Campbell gave themselves an eighteen-minute window for each job. Eighteen minutes to orient themselves to time and place, find something worth stealing, and get back before that window slammed closed forever.

But it was an arbitrary amount of time, not an actual estimate based on anything resembling science. Hell, it was a *Jurassic Park* reference, not anything to risk their lives over.

"We have enough," Lindy said, trying to sound less anxious than she felt. "I'm going back."

She didn't wait for an answer, she didn't wait for him. Nobody, not even a scruffy-faced scoundrel with a heart of fool's gold and eyes of topaz, was worth getting trapped so far from home.

But Campbell followed her, out the back door and into the alley behind the shop. That's what they did, he followed her and she followed him, ever since the day they met.

Relief flooded through Lindy's body to see that faint glimmer in the night. One day, their luck would run out. But not today.

Time worked differently in the other world, but it worked.

Someone could walk through a portal from the 1930s and meet a herd of brachiosaurus stampeding in from 150 million years ago. But today was always today, and tomorrow always came after that. This place, this waystation between times, ran on its own internal clock.

Sometimes Lindy wondered if more time might pass here than they actually spent in the timeline on Earth, but it was hardly noticeable. She would, however, add another page of data to her notebook and keep track, just in case.

"I want to get some clocks next time we go somewhere more modern," she told Campbell as they walked through the prehistoric forest. "Real accurate ones."

He gave a nod, and snatched up a fallen branch to swing while they walked.

Of all the wondrous and unbelievable things she had seen over the past weeks, Campbell's ability to be completely and utterly uninterested in this parallel world was the most fascinating. Sure, he had marveled at it in the beginning, occasionally stopped to stare at a particularly strange dinosaur, but he made it painfully obvious that he was not a scientist and didn't care to understand this new world they discovered so long as he could use it to get rich.

Not discovered, Lindy reminded herself as they came upon the small settlement on the banks of a wide and winding river that cut through the landscape. This world already had people living there when they arrived. It wasn't theirs to claim.

"Anything good?" one of the merchants called out.

Campbell held up his bag. "Got some nice rotary phones, if you got the electricity."

The merchant laughed, wiping his hands as he came around the front of his food stall. The handful of people who lived there came from various times across history, but the settlement itself could be described as early medieval in terms of technology, though there was talk of starting some hydroelectric projects.

"No, fresh out of electricity today."

"Any of that tonic you had last time?" Lindy asked. "For headaches?"

"My husband is out picking the plants as we speak; check back in a couple days. As for today, how about some fruit?"

Campbell kept walking. Lindy paused long enough to trade some trinkets for a bag of small, red berries that didn't have a proper name. They had gone extinct long before humans evolved, a secret delicacy known only to prehistory, and tasted rather like kiwis.

"Might be the last of those I'll be able to get you for a while," the merchant told her. "Think the baryonyx up by where they grow are starting to nest."

"Eh. They don't bother me, maybe I'll get my own, thanks."

"What don't bother you?" Campbell asked as she caught up to him.

Lindy poured a generous amount of berries into his hand when he held it out. "Baryonyx."

"Are they the ones...?" He mimed a long snout and tyrannosaurus-like hands. At her confirmation, he just shook his head. "You gotta stop with them, Lin, they—"

"They eat fish," she argued. The same comfortable old argument they used to have back home about stray cats, just on a slightly larger scale.

"And geese eat bread. Doesn't stop them attacking if you bother them."

Lindy popped a berry in her mouth. "If we domesticate them, maybe we could ride them."

"You're joking. I know you're joking, so I'm ignoring you." He squinted at her, as if trying to determine if she truly was joking.

She wasn't entirely sure.

It was autumn. Lindy supposed it had been autumn already, the last time they went to that precious slice of Vermont in 1998 they called home, but the season had properly settled in now.

The air had that undefinable crisp quality that brought the taste of apple cider to her tongue and made Lindy long for a nice and frustrating evening lost in a corn maze. Peeking out through the barn doors, she saw splashes of yellow and orange beginning to take over the trees of the Roman family farm.

It wasn't much, but it was home. She worried how much she would miss it as she reflexively ran her finger along the heart carved on the old wood door.

"We could stay this time. Not here," she said, indicating the farm, the town, Vermont. "But...here." She made a vague gesture at this universe. "Get the money from camp, come back here, and run away to another life."

Campbell considered it as he gathered his wares and loaded his gun. She hated seeing him with that gun. It made him look like the criminal he was, and she didn't like thinking about that.

"Maybe," Campbell said. He was lying, but Lindy suspected he believed it.

After giving her a quick kiss, he slipped out of the barn, promising to be back by dusk.

Lindy did not follow him. She couldn't. Too many people would recognize her here.

And so she made herself comfortable and waited, studying her notes in the barely discernable illumination given off by the rip in space and time.

This portal, the one that saved them, had been open for weeks now, allowing travel between this world and the other. But it would close, sooner or later it would close, and she wanted to be on the right side of it when it did.

If there was a pattern dictating where, when, and for how long a portal would open, Lindy couldn't find it. Not enough data. Even in the other world—and even if it wasn't theirs to claim, she thought they really should think of a name for it at some point—portals were more of a novelty than an everyday occurrence, and didn't give her much opportunity for study.

On a whim, she flipped to a blank page in her notebook and started listing all of the strange creature sightings and unexplained disappearances she could remember off the top of her head. Maybe the lost colony of Roanoke had gone through a portal, or maybe that famous film purporting to show a sasquatch actually showed some extinct hominid who had wandered into the modern era.

She couldn't prove any of it, but it was at least more data to play with, the start of making some sort of scientific sense out of this.

Campbell came back late that night, late enough that Lindy had begun to worry he'd been arrested but not so late for her to consider cutting and running before they came for her, too.

Not seriously, anyway.

"Big score?" she asked quietly, as if somehow afraid she would break the stillness of the night, wake her parents sleeping in that little house way across the farm. She assumed they were there, anyway; all the times she and Campbell had been back, she never went to see how they were, if they missed her, if they were even looking.

"Big enough," he said, but there was something about his infectious grin that intrigued and concerned Lindy in equal amounts.

"What?" she asked, returning his grin.

Campbell stepped closer, wrapped his arms around her, and said those three little words every woman wanted to hear.

"One last job."

Here they were again. Months later, another world, the same old story.

This job felt wrong, just like the first time Campbell had put a gun in her hand and told her they were going to rob a bank. Morally wrong, but dangerous wrong, too. Not just because they could get killed, either.

It was crossing a line they couldn't uncross, putting a target on their backs and shifting their moral compasses until they became the kind of people who would do this sort of thing without a second thought.

And just like the first time, Lindy wanted to believe that the first time would be the only time. She wanted to, pretended to, but couldn't.

"Who's the fence again?"

Campbell waited a moment to answer, intently watching through the leaves as if making sure the baryonyx pair hadn't noticed them. "We can trust him."

"Not what I asked."

Whether there was an answer that would satisfy her misgivings about the situation, she couldn't say. Purchasing a black market dinosaur egg from time-traveling criminals certainly didn't sound like the activities of a trustworthy person, but still. She would prefer knowing exactly who Campbell had told about this world, and how much.

"He won't sell us out," Campbell assured her, or attempted to. He patted her arm urgently and pointed. The female was leaving, probably for food. They did that, trusted each other to care for the nest.

If a tyrannosaurus was a monster truck, baryonyx was an Italian sports car. Sleek and streamlined, larger than a horse but somehow still managing to look small and compact. The pair nesting in the clearing even had the colors right, deep red with black racing stripes on either side of their long snouts.

Lindy had never seen them being particularly vicious, just snapping at other individuals trying to hunt fish at the same spot along the river. But the female tended to be less patient than her mate; if the last week of observation had taught Lindy anything, it was that she would rather deal with the male.

"Wish me luck," she whispered when the female was gone, kissing her crossed fingers so her luck wouldn't run out before carefully walking out of the hiding place.

She glanced at the male dinosaur, acknowledging him with a small nod, as she started gathering berries near the treeline just as she had every day that week. By now, the baryonyxes were accustomed to her presence enough that the male no longer sat directly on the nest to protect the eggs from her, but rather stalked the perimeter of his territory, looking for danger or finding new leaves to add to the nest.

"I'm sorry about this," Lindy said when he stopped to sniff the air about a dozen yards away.

He showed no indication of understanding her, but there was still an intelligence in the way he looked at Lindy, tilting his feathered head as if studying her.

Lindy popped a berry into her mouth and tossed one toward the dinosaur. He tracked the movement through the air and across the ground, lowering his body until his front claws nearly scraped the grass, then straightened up in annoyance upon realizing it was nothing of interest.

As casually as she could manage, Lindy moved closer to the nest, taking care to seem like the berries were her only concern. Was there even a nest there? Oh, how funny, she hadn't noticed.

She was close enough now to see the oblong eggs peeking through the leaves covering them. Three of them, laid just days ago and presumably nowhere close to hatching. If she could see inside, it would likely just be yolk and albumin and the microscopic promise of a dinosaur.

She looked at the baryonyx, at the nest, at Campbell. Could she get an egg in her bag and get back to Campbell before the father noticed it was missing?

"It's not fair to you," she said, because the dinosaurs were used to her chatter by now, and because it would cover up any suspicious sounds as she stepped closer to the eggs. "It's not your fault I fell for a guy too charming for his own good. Or my own good."

The dinosaur—Lindy had started thinking of him as Paul, and his mate as Amanda, after her cousin and his wife—glanced at her a couple times as she neared the nest, but she had established herself as a herbivore and he didn't seem to think of her as a threat.

Stealing the egg didn't particularly scare Lindy, not as much as what would happen after. Would the buyer let the egg die and use it as some sort of status symbol, or try to hatch it? She almost hoped for the first, as she couldn't imagine the poor thing trying to thrive all alone in a world not meant for it.

Maybe Paul moved with the practiced silence of an apex predator, maybe Lindy's heart was beating too loud in her ears as she bent down and started moving the nesting materials out of the way. Either way, she didn't hear him until the sudden warning snarl.

She straightened up, turned around slowly with her hands up like the criminal she was.

The baryonyx stood just feet away, his neck bent so he could look down his long snout at her. His mouth was open slightly, and while his teeth may have been designed by evolution to eat fish, he was so large that Lindy doubted it would matter. He could easily take most of her body in his massive jaws, end her with a single snap.

Only then, with the dinosaur between her and Campbell, did she realize the irony. No, not irony. Hypocrisy.

Just the other day, he had lectured her about the dangers of going near the breeding grounds to pick berries. But now that it would earn him money, now that it was *his* idea, he was encouraging her not just to go near the breeding grounds but to steal an egg right out of a nest.

Only then, with the dinosaur between her and Campbell, did Lindy realize she trusted the dinosaur more. At least Paul's intentions were clear: protect his family. Campbell . . . Campbell just wanted to protect Campbell.

"I'm not going to hurt you," she whispered. "I'm not going to hurt your eggs."

Campbell always yelled at her for making friends with stray cats, said they would scratch or bite. But animals liked her, trusted her. Maybe that gave her more confidence than was wise, but Lindy would rather risk her safety on her own bad decision instead of someone else's.

She took a step back, around the nest, and then another when the dinosaur made no move to attack. She took another step away from everything she knew, from any chance of going home and having a normal life.

She took another step away from Campbell.

And then she turned, and she ran.

The Good, the Bad, and the Utahraptor

No one could say for sure exactly when the dinosaurs started appearing outside the little mining town of Hell Creek, nor where they'd come from. Rumors of cattle found dead with long slashes across their hides went back to the 1850s, but the raptors had been showing up more often in the last few decades, even coming into town when food got scarce.

People said they came from under the ground, down from the depths of Hell itself, and that the miners' dynamite woke 'em up. Rosita's abuela said they were descended from some kind of feathered lizard god.

Rosita didn't particularly care about any of that. She just wanted to ride one.

They weren't so different from horses, she reckoned. They were about the height of Ellie, her daddy's piebald mare, just with two legs instead of four, and she'd been riding Ellie since before she could walk. She'd even helped her brothers break wild mustangs a couple times.

And so maybe the raptors had knives for claws and mouths fulla sharp teeth, and maybe they were fiercer predators than even the mountain lions and bears. But people had domesticated the wolf, hadn't they? How were raptors any different?

Far as Rosita knew, no one had ever ridden a raptor. No one had even touched one, at least not anyone who'd lived to tell about it. What a sight she'd be, all dressed up and sitting atop an iridescent murder-bird while she did her trick shots.

"

The Wild West shows would *have* to hire her then. She'd get out of Hell Creek, see the world, and send her pay back home. The farms and mines weren't turning much of a profit since the raptors started killing the cattle and scaring folks who tried to go to the mines.

So Rosita set out early one morning, rope in one hand and Daddy's Colt revolver in the other 'cause she weren't no fool. If things didn't go well, she'd have to defend herself. A dead daughter wouldn't earn a cent on the show circuit, not unless they mummified her, and Rosita didn't think her mama'd go for that.

She wore her brother's hand-me-down boots and set her best gray Stetson on her head as she hiked out to the craggy red rocks on the edge of town. A pack congregated out in the open like they owned the place, because nothing was foolish enough to go messing with them.

Rosita stood a ways back, examining the pack as they fought over the remains of something that might have been a deer. Good—they'd be full and less likely to attack.

Or so she hoped.

Their faces looked like a gila monster's, scaly with yellow eyes and gaping mouths, but a coating of feathers covered their bodies and made 'em look all soft and beautiful. Most of the half-dozen were a gray-blue with a purple sheen, but one, standing on the periphery like she didn't quite fit in, had pinkish highlights that gleamed in the sunlight.

"That's the one," Rosita whispered. But she stayed put. It was easy to think she'd be successful if she didn't actually try it, if she stayed far enough back that the raptors looked like colorful little turkeys.

When Rosita was a young'n, the sheriff had brought a dead raptor to the school to show the kids, to teach 'em they was right to be afraid. She'd never forget the sheer mass of it, half a ton of muscle and razors. Even dead, the beast had dominated the room, the threat of disembowelment lingering in its glassy eyes.

She knew she shoulda turned and ran back to town, practiced her trick riding with Ellie and found some other way to make it into the show, but she tightened her grip on the rope anyway and slowly made her way toward the pack.

The pink one saw her first, her head turning sharply and her gaze meeting Rosita's. Her long back legs flexed as she crouched, looking ready to spring into action.

A wave of panic went through Rosita; what if the deer hadn't been enough food for the lot of them? She'd never outrun one on foot. Maybe she shoulda brought Ellie, but her parents couldn't stand to lose their best horse *and* their second-best daughter. Not on the same day.

The raptor took a slow step forward, then another. By now the two were close enough that Rosita could see a slash of red across the animal's neck. Injured, probably in a fight with another raptor.

"You ain't nothing to them," Rosita said softly. "Are ya?"

The raptor tilted her head and gave a little warble.

"They cast you out? On account of you not being a good hunter, not being pretty like your sister?"

Only a dozen yards separated Rosita and the raptor. She'd never been so close to a living one before, but from this distance she could see the animal's chest expand with every deep breath, and the sickle claws made for tearing flesh.

Rosita took a step back. The raptor kept coming.

Wrapping her fingers around the Colt's grip, Rosita wondered what would happen if she shot it. She wouldn't miss, but would the sound draw the others or scare them off? Would she have time to get away?

She backed slowly into the shade of a rocky outcropping as the raptor advanced, and felt the cool sandstone against her back. Nowhere to run. She started spinning her rope the way her daddy had taught her. The raptor's attention was briefly drawn to the circle of rope turning overhead, and Rosita let it fly.

The raptor cried out in panic as the loop slipped over her neck, and she jerked, inadvertently tightening the lasso. The fibers burned Rosita's palm as the raptor pulled at the slack, calling out in alarm and distress.

Rosita's blood turned to ice at the sight of the pack at high alert, all eyes looking directly at her. She dropped the rope and pulled back the hammer of her revolver. She prided herself on taking quick shots, but her life had never depended on it before.

She took a breath, steadied her aim—

A low whistle sounded in the distance. The train was coming into town.

Every raptor swivelled toward the sound, the leader called back with a chirp, and off the pack ran to chase the locomotive.

The raptors easily kept pace with the train as it slowed on its way into Hell Creek. They woulda followed it all the way to the station, but the passengers didn't like that so much and had taken to tossing hunks of meat off the train to appease the critters.

It'd become a big to-do in recent months, with people riding out to the mines just to see the raptors racing the train, and ain't nobody would dare try to rob a train that came with its own security raptors.

Rosita rode out to watch, studying the stretch of track where they threw the meat. Smooth terrain, no big rocks or cacti. When the train wasn't around and the raptors were off terrorizing farms, she and Ellie practiced matching the speeds. Then she brought in her brother's wildest stallion to stand in for the raptor, and they spent weeks doing the most dangerous stunt she'd ever tried.

It all worked in theory. Now to add the raptors.

Ellie seemed to know this wasn't another training run, and held her ears flat against her head as they waited for the train.

"Me too, mija," Rosita whispered, running her hands through Ellie's mane. Would the horse act the same around raptors as she did with the other horse? Would she run away to safety like they practiced? Would she even let herself be ridden so close to a vicious predator?

The train's whistle announced the impending moment of truth. Rosita squeezed her legs and leaned forward, gently urging Ellie toward the tracks.

They timed it perfectly, with Ellie breaking into a run as the train started to slow, matching the pace of the raptor pack. Between the wind and the roar of the locomotive, Rosita couldn't hear a thing. And she loved it.

This was exactly the kind of stunt they did in the traveling Wild West shows. Horses and riders racing trains, defying death, maybe even reenacting great battles of the War Between the States.

The meat throwing began.

One by one, the raptors caught a piece and fell back from the pack to devour it by the tracks, until only the pink one remained, her stronger and bigger packmates having muscled her out of the way. She still had a bit of the rope looped over her neck, though the end had been chewed short and ragged.

Rosita waved her hat to the folks in the train, the signal for them to stop feeding the raptors, and edged Ellie closer. At first the horse balked, so Rosita waited and tried again. The raptor had to smell them approaching, but the entirety of her attention was on the train window and she paid them no mind.

Ellie and the pink raptor ran in almost in tandem, hooves and claws pounding the earth, mane and feathers flapping. Their heads and backs were nearly level; Rosita couldn't have planned it better.

She slipped her feet out of the stirrups and pulled her knees up under her, no easy feat on a galloping beast made of muscle.

No turning back now.

She took a shaky breath and leapt to her feet. The wind took her hat, but Rosita had no time to mourn its loss. The next minute or so was pure chaos and instinct.

She threw herself off Ellie, trusting the horse to flee to safety. Her chin struck the raptor's head as she tried to grab onto the feathered critter.

Then came the pain in her chest. Sky and ground and sky again tumbled over each other, limbs crushing against limbs as raptor and rider lost both their balance and the fight against momentum. Rosita held onto the rope for all she was worth, and the two of them skidded on the ground as the train sped away.

Next she knew, Rosita was on her back and a claw was passing just inches from her face. She took that as a good sign; the raptor must have been disoriented, else she'd have been dead.

Rosita forced herself to her feet. The raptor hunched down, ready to strike but breathing heavy.

"I'm unarmed, mija," Rosita said quietly, trying to keep her voice steady even though she was pretty damn sure she'd broken at least one rib. She'd been so preoccupied with whether she *could* ride a raptor that she didn't stop to think if she *should*. "I can't fight back. But I don't think you're in much of a state to fight yourself."

Her own injuries were from the tussle, but the raptor's were in various stages of healing. Cuts and bites on her neck and back, a patch of missing feathers, a forearm that didn't bend quite right. . . .

"You can kill me if you want, but it won't make them accept you."

The raptor tilted her head to one side. Rosita wasn't so foolish as to think she actually understood, but they were both clever girls. Even if the raptor didn't know Rosita was trying to reason with her, the human's nonsensical chattering seemed to at least convey the absence of a threat.

"Or," Rosita said, taking a tentative step forward, "you can let me ride you outta this town and you and I will make something of ourselves."

The raptor watched her warily, toothy mouth open in a soft hiss, but made no move to strike. Rosita reached her hand out and gave the raptor's scaly nose a quick pat before retreating.

It was hardly as impressive as riding one, but she'd just become the first person she knew of who'd touched a living raptor and kept all their limbs.

That seemed like a good first step.

A Tale of Two Citipati

Two portals opened simultaneously in a nameless land beyond time. Two portals opened on Earth, a century and a half apart.

Each with a story of its own to tell, history repeating, rhyming, completely different songs with the same meter. "Amazing Grace" sung to the tune of the *Gilligan's Island* theme and vice versa.

Two dinosaurs saw the opening of the portals. A mating pair of citipati, bonded for life and parting ways. They were nameless as the land, but we will call them Grace and Gilligan.

Grace's portal was expected, welcome. Exactly what the residents of Hell Creek had been waiting for.

Still, when the deputy rode into town announcing it was open, Rosita couldn't bring herself to feel anything but sadness.

She had been the first to ride a raptor, but not the last. For the better part of a decade, human and dinosaur coexisted in this quiet little town spitting distance from the middle of nowhere. It was their normal.

But with America expanding west, the middle of nowhere was fast becoming the frontier of somewhere. If outsiders found out about the raptors, if they found the doorway that regularly opened into that other world, it would be another place to conquer and ruin.

The dinosaurs had to go back, and nearly half the town, her brother and his family included, decided to go with.

"She's used to being around folks," Rosita explained again as everyone gathered at the portal. She stroked her raptor's feathers that gleamed iridescent pink in the setting sun. They never did get to ride in Wild West shows. "Might not know how to hunt anymore."

Her sister smiled at her through tears. "You don't got to apologize. You've always wanted to get out of this place."

"And you've always been the favorite daughter."

"It's sad you think that's true." Her sister held her hand for a moment, kissed the raptor on the snout, and went back to stand with the others who were staying behind.

One by one, human and dinosaur stepped through the portal, every possibility waiting for them.

Rosita was meant to be the first, but she and her raptor busied themselves chasing down Grace and ushering her back into her world. Though not much smaller than the predatory utahraptor, Grace the citipati allowed herself to be herded without much fuss, and soon the only evidence of her presence were birdlike footprints and a handful of white feathers.

Rosita followed her through the portal, the first and last person to ever ride a dinosaur in Hell Creek.

Gilligan's portal, and Gilligan himself, came as quite the surprise.

Where Hell Creek was nowhere becoming somewhere, the Yellowstone Medieval Faire marked the end of something becoming nothing. The last event of the season for the performers and vendors who would soon remove the armor and corsets and funny little hats in favor of the equally ridiculous costumes and funny little hats of various retail jobs across the Billings area.

Marcus noticed the creature first. Still draped in his maroon and gold robes—made from only the finest silks and furs and jewels one could buy at Joann Fabrics—the young man frowned in confusion at the fluffy white dinosaur tentatively walking some distance down the abandoned midway.

"Ravi left already?" he asked the others, the last dozen or so still packing up stalls and collecting their things in the dwindling daylight.

"I believe so," his sister said, distracted slightly by the task of ensuring everything in her costume tent was labeled correctly as she put it away. "Got called into work tomorrow. You know how it is at Electrum."

Strange. That certainly looked like one of Ravi's intricate, over-sized dragon puppets.

"I shall return," Marcus declared, setting off toward the creature.

He didn't have to get much closer to realize he was looking at a flesh and blood animal. Ostrich, his brain decided, despite being in Montana, despite knowing ostriches didn't have head crests or long, whipping tails.

Marcus and Gilligan stared at each other curiously. Not an ostrich.

"Hey guys," Marcus called out, and Gilligan spooked, turning and running back the way he came.

When Marcus took off after him, his sister and friends followed out of curiosity and perhaps a bit of concern. And there, behind the grandstand, a dozen people in various vaguely medieval outfits found themselves gathered before a portal.

"You're not seriously going through?" Marcus's sister asked when he stepped toward it.

"Just a quick look," he said.

"Howdy."

"Good morrow."

And so began the relationship between the two groups that emerged from the portals and found themselves in a strange and wondrous land without a name.

One of the portals closed almost immediately. Not the one to Hell Creek but the other, the one to wherever those fancy folks had come from. Maybe it would open again, maybe they were trapped, maybe they would try to escape and end up in Hell Creek.

Rosita didn't know enough about temporal mechanics and butterfly effects to say exactly why, but messing with the way of things and letting them into a time they didn't belong just felt dangerous.

Back home, the people who stayed were planning on putting up a building around the area where the portal tended to appear. Hiding it from outsiders, maybe even future generations of citizens, anything to protect the secret and this world that didn't ask to be the newest frontier.

Rosita hadn't thought they would need to do it on this side as well.

"We got to protect the doorway," she told the others, taking charge since nobody else seemed keen to.

Gabriel, an older gentleman who had become the town veterinarian on account of being the only person brave or perhaps foolish enough to take care of the raptors, pointed at the king and his subjects. "What about them?"

The answer, at least to Rosita, was obvious. "We got to protect them, too."

When it became clear the other group was truly from the American Old West, Marcus gathered his people and, still playing king, issued a decree.

"It's like *Star Trek*," he began.

"I thought it was like *Jurassic Park*," his sister said.

"*Jurassic Park III*," corrected Nina, one of the jousters. "Because no one is coming to save us and I really wish Jeff Goldblum was here."

"It's like *Star Trek*," Marcus continued. "We are from a more advanced civilization, it wouldn't be right for us to influence their society. Why not let them believe we really are from the middle ages until we find a way home?"

And so the performers and vendors began their awkward and anachronistic farce. Their costumes, historically accurate only if one squinted, were modeled after vastly different times and places that vaguely fell under the "Medieval and/or Renaissance" umbrella, and Vince who ran the cotton candy stand insisted on adding "ye olde" before every noun, but the cowboys seemed to buy the act.

That was all that mattered. Protecting the timeline that was clearly already a little damaged.

They built the town together with supplies brought from Hell Creek. Just a few buildings, a paddock for the raptors.

They named the world together. Avalonia. Marcus's suggestion, after the island of legend, with Rosita changing the ending so it sounded prettier.

And it worked at first.

The town grew, more houses and a stable and a well for fresh drinking water. The cowboys taught the knights to ride raptors, so they could explore farther in search of a portal home.

They were a peculiar little mismatched community brought together by fate and a pair of citipati, but it worked.

And then it didn't.

New Hell Creek wasn't the only human settlement in the nameless land now called Avalonia, but the others were all some distance away and so strangers were rare. Especially strangers like her.

"Forgive me for staring," Rosita said, marveling at the faded turquoise ends of the woman's ginger braid. "But I ain't seen someone with hair like that before."

The woman smiled up at her, keeping her distance but seeming oddly comfortable with the notion of being in such close proximity to a raptor. "Forgive me for staring, but I didn't know they would let you ride them."

Rosita nodded, silently taking in the stranger's clothing. Denim pants long enough only to cover her thighs, a blouse with patterns brighter and more intricate than her mama's wildest calico print, and shoes she didn't have a name for as her vocabulary did not yet include "Chuck Taylor."

The woman pointed to her head, indicating Rosita's hat. "When is home for you?"

Rosita gave the date they had left Hell Creek and added, "Home is here now."

"Same. Only I'm from a century later." Frowning thoughtfully, the woman asked, "How are you guys doing? We don't have much in my town, but we're working on figuring out electricity."

"You'd help us?"

"If you teach me to ride a dinosaur," the woman said with a grin. "I'm Lindy, by the way."

Like the citipati, Lindy was one half of a bonded pair parting ways. The same tune with different lyrics, it just so happened that the Gilligan to her Grace was at that time miles away, staring up at Marcus.

"Damn," he muttered. "My girl was right, you can ride dinosaurs."

"Dragon, my good sir," Marcus corrected, projecting his voice as if announcing the winning jouster. "I know not of this dinosaur of which you speak. 'Tis the tamed spawn of the dragon that lay siege to my kingdom."

The dinosaur gave the tiniest snarl, his long claws digging into the dirt as he tightened his muscles.

Campbell was hardly convinced, or intimidated. "I deal in antiquities. Middle ages, admittedly not my specialty. I could point out a couple incongruous costuming details, more if your angry little friend let me get a closer look, but we are conversing in modern English right now so...." He pretended to think for a moment. "Yeah, I think you know exactly what dinosaurs are."

Rather than be annoyed at the deception, Campbell seemed infinitely fascinated by Marcus. He walked alongside the king and his dinosaur, making conversation as they scouted the surrounding area for potential dangers or resources.

At the mention of the portal to Hell Creek, something changed in his demeanor that went unnoticed by Marcus but made the dinosaur tense up.

"Listen, I've got a semi-stable wormhole myself. I wish I could get you all the way home but I can get you as far as 1998."

For the first time since getting trapped in this godforsaken wilderness, something resembling hope fluttered in Marcus's heart. "Verily?"

"Absolutely. Although you would still be a regular guy in a regular world."

"Is there another option?" Marcus asked, frowning.

Campbell shrugged. "I'm just saying, whoever controls access to the portals has the power around here. You get me antiques from the 1800s, I take them to the future and sell them, I'll bring you back whatever you want to help build your kingdom. I will bring you a throne, your majesty."

Entire history books could be written about what transpired next. Indeed, each side would write their own, the accuracy dependent on who wrote them and why, but the facts were these:

New Hell Creek existed entirely to keep the portal secret. Rosita and her people left everything they had ever known to secure the other end of the doorway connecting Avalonia and Earth, prevent people and creatures from going through in either direction. Of course Marcus's requests to access it were declined.

He continued to insist. Told his people it was the way home.

But if it was the way home, they asked, why were the people from Hell Creek not letting them leave?

Marcus needed a scapegoat, he found one in Lindy. This stranger, he said, was turning everyone against him. And like that, she became the enemy. She, and the futuristic ideals she brought with her.

They weren't so far off from his own ideals, but the lie had gone on too long now, he couldn't tell the truth. He needed to blame something other than himself.

The townsfolk parted ways.

New Hell Creek grew slowly but steadily, gates open to anyone who needed somewhere to call home. Marcus built walls around a false kingdom he jokingly named after a prehistoric camel. Cowboys riding dinosaurs denied the existence of the portal, knights on dragons told themselves they were important and Camelops would one day rival Camelot. The next generation inherited those lies as truth, the reasons for their animosity forgotten as time marched on in the realm beyond time.

"We want to use their portal" became "they won't help us survive" became "those people want to destroy everything we have built here."

And "we must protect the timeline" became "they want to steal our resources" became "those people want to destroy everything we have built here."

One town became two territories fighting a war that would outlive Marcus and Rosita's generation.

Somewhere in the land now known as Avalonia, however, there was hope. Somewhere, somehow, the two citipati had found each other again.

Their mating calls would always be completely different songs, awful and chaotic when sung together, but they had the same meter. But the songs of their hatchlings, that was a symphony.

Pirates of the Cambrian

Amelia was amazing through it all. As if there was any doubt. She'd always been an amazing, absolute spitfire from the moment I joined her World Flight. If I could have anyone by my side when everything seemed hopeless, it would be her.

Not sure the feeling was mutual.

The irony of the situation was that Amelia selected me for the job because her previous navigator, Harry Manning, couldn't plot an accurate enough course. She said I had the skills she needed, I was the man who would see her home safely.

"You know where Harry Manning is right now?" I asked softly, leaning my head back against a tree. "Because I do."

Amelia looked up from her notes, or what we could save of them before the ocean consumed the Electra. The firelight played on her short hair that had never been particularly styled but had become absolutely unruly over the last day and a half. She seemed annoyed, not at me necessarily, more at the absurdity of the question. "And where would that be?"

"Earth."

Now she seemed annoyed at me. At the hopelessness in my voice, anyway. "We're still on Earth."

We weren't. The trees and birds on the island defied recognition, we had both seen glimpses of monstrous things in the water, and the stars.... "The stars aren't ours, Millie."

"Different latitude," she said stubbornly. "We went further off course than previously thought, could be in the Antarctic. Have you ever seen the stars from the Antarctic?"

With a tilt of my head, I reluctantly granted her that point. "Shouldn't it be colder?"

"Arthur Conan Doyle," was her only response before returning to her notes.

I scratched at the scruff trying desperately to become a beard on my chin, wondering how Sherlock Holmes fit into this.

Oh. Amelia meant *The Lost World*. Little pocket of Earth that didn't follow the rules of climate or extinction.

I chose not to mention that the Electra wouldn't have had enough fuel to get us far enough for the stars to change. I didn't necessarily think she believed it anyway, just needed an explanation so she could focus on surviving instead of wondering where or why we were.

"Need to reinforce that," she said, pointing with her pencil at our rudimentary shelter. "It's sufficient, but I worry if it rains."

"Tomorrow," I agreed, rapping my knuckles against the tree behind me; the nice big leaves would make fine roofing material. "First thing."

Amelia pointed at the jungle next. "I thought I'd explore in the morning. See what resources we have while we wait for rescue."

A little way out from shore, moonlight illuminated a group of long-necked creatures surfacing for air beneath alien constellations.

Rescue wasn't coming.

The ship came over the horizon with the rising sun, almost like she was dragging the light of day behind her like some sort of mythological chariot.

Amelia and I whooped and screamed, hugging each other as sobs of relief shook our bodies. The unfamiliar stars, the prehistoric monsters . . . I couldn't explain them, and I didn't care. Never in my life have I been so overjoyed to be wrong. We were on Earth, about to be rescued, nothing else mattered.

We started waving, shouting, long before they could see or hear us. I added kindling to our signal fire, and the ship drew closer, closer. I could make out the details now, I could—

The ship didn't make sense.

She was shaped like a luxury liner, though she couldn't have been more than a hundred feet. The *Queen Mary* in miniature. But a forest of masts and sails gave her the most peculiar silhouette, and then there was the flag.

Black, with a white skull over top of two wicked, curved talons.

"Pirates?" Amelia whispered.

Pirates.

Amelia and I grabbed some large pieces of wood to use as improvised weapons if need be, and we moved into the treeline while the ship sent a smaller boat to shore. I don't know what either of us expected besides the worst, but the crew disembarked in a casual manner, laughing and joking with each other, and then a woman called out to us.

"Whoever you are, we've taken no side in the war and don't aim to harm you! Come out and say ahoy or stay out of our way, makes no difference to us, but any violence will be met in kind and threefold!"

Motioning for Amelia to stay put and knowing she would ignore me anyway, I took a few steps toward the beach. It wasn't a big island, nowhere to run, so I didn't think it would make much of a difference if they did mean harm.

The crew was like the ship: they gave the impression of piracy but not in any cohesive or threatening fashion. I almost wondered if we had crossed paths with a budget production of *Penzance*.

I had no trouble identifying the captain. It wasn't the way she looked or talked, though scars of past battles haunted her face and her long frock coat gave her the air of authority, and the others tended to immediately comply with any order she made in that rather pretty Irish accent.

It was the way she held herself, the almost spiteful confidence daring anybody not to take her seriously. She reminded me of Amelia.

"When you've decided to stop staring and introduce yourselves," she called out between consulting a piece of parchment and directing her crew to unload supplies from the ship, "do let me know."

Amelia had already started toward the beach before the captain spoke, muttering "Feel ridiculous, just standing here waiting," but walked with more purpose in her step now. I kept pace but still felt like I was following somehow.

She extended her hand in greeting, diplomatic and with only a hint of her usual friendliness. "Amelia—"

"Earhart," the captain said in disbelief, taking Amelia's hand in both of hers and grinning. "Well, we came in search of missing treasure so it looks like we're on the right track!" The last part was directed at her crew, who gave a small cheer.

Amelia and I shared a look.

"You've heard of me." A statement more than a question, and I could see Amelia relax slightly. Wherever we were, whatever had happened, the world still made a little sense.

"'Heard of you.'" The captain cackled. It was a sharp sound, like the crack of a whip, but her smile made it somehow endearing. "Of course I've heard of you. My dear, you are Amelia Louise—"

"Mary."

"I took a guess. Even better, love the name Mary." Finally releasing Amelia's hand, the captain gestured at her enthusiastically. "Amelia Mary Earhart! One of the most famous women in history. Who hasn't heard of you? Centuries after your disappearance, they still talk about you."

Disappearance.

So much information packed into that single word, all of which I saw Amelia process before it hit me properly that we weren't going home.

"They don't talk about *you*," Annie informed me, letting her first mate take the lead so she could fall into step beside me as we began our journey into the jungle.

I can't say that fact was particularly shocking, but the way it gave my stomach a slight twinge of something resembling jealousy took me by surprise. "Sounds about right."

"Does it?" the captain asked, nimbly stepping over exposed roots without so much as glancing at her feet.

Anne Bonny—"Annie to my friends, 'that bitch' to my enemies, your choice"—seemed pleasant enough. For a pirate, anyway, which I assumed necessitated a different set of standards.

She had done her best to explain the bizarre land out of time Amelia and I had found ourselves in, caught us up on some war between kings and cowboys, and provided food and fresh changes of clothing. Yes, it's true we weren't given the choice to decline joining her crew as they ventured into the jungle in search of treasure, but her attitude about it resembled that of a Southern aunt saying she won't take no for an answer when offering dessert, and I wasn't even completely certain we had been taken prisoner. Invited without consent, more like, and she claimed she would help us settle in this world if we helped find her treasure.

"No offense intended," she had said, "but I'm not leaving you unattended with my ship. Can't risk you getting curious and poking around. Rexy is too good a guard dog and I'm sick of cleaning up blood."

But what was she getting at now, telling me history forgot me and questioning how I felt about it? I liked her well enough, but I was still quite a ways from trusting her.

"Compared to Amelia?" I answered finally, gesturing to that amazing and peculiar woman who had confidently charged to the front of the group, her head on a swivel trying to take in every new plant and bird call. "Yes, ma'am, I am quite content being a nobody in her shadow."

Annie snatched a stick off the ground, idly brandishing it like a sword as if she didn't have a cutlass and several smaller blades on her belt. "Nothing wrong with being a nobody," she agreed. "Just ask Odysseus. It's why I've got a crew of them."

I frowned. "I don't follow."

Suddenly, Annie's hand was blocking my field of vision, forcing me to stumble to a stop. "Can you tell me anything about my crew? Describe any of them in detail? Anything about their personality?"

I couldn't. "What are you getting at?" I asked, ducking away from her hand in mild annoyance.

"Everyone looks at me," Annie said, gesturing at herself from head to toe with a sweeping motion. "And that's by design. I'm bold, I'm famous, I'm a threat. Not to mention gorgeous, don't tell me you weren't thinking it but remember, when it comes to ships and partners, I don't mind a top mast but I much prefer a motorboat."

I didn't know how to respond, and I was quite all right with that.

"But I'm *not* the threat. It's my crew, the ones you didn't even know were there, that you need to worry about."

I felt the need to glance behind me. Nothing but lush greenery. "Why are you telling me this?"

Annie just grinned and started catching up to the rest of the group. "Amelia Mary Earhart! I've questions about your most fascinating life...."

"What's the treasure, then?" Amelia asked a little while later when Annie stopped to consult her map of the island.

Now that I knew to look, I couldn't help but notice the slight difference in clothing we had been provided. Where I was the picture of a generic pirate in a faded shirt with blue stripes and trousers so nondescript that it would be a disservice to the English language to waste words describing them, Amelia was the portrait of a pirate queen.

Her shirt was clean and crisp white, her pants comfortably tailored and reminiscent of her aviator attire. Her jacket wasn't nearly as grand as Annie's, but it made a statement.

"The treasure," Annie said, crouching to examine the unrolled parchment from a different angle, "is the only thing in this world that matters."

She frowned, staring at the map and muttering to herself. The word "east" came up several times.

"You don't have compasses?" I asked.

"World is weird. Magnetic field is about as trustworthy as a . . ."

Annie trailed off, the map taking up all of her attention. "...un-trustworthy thing."

One of her crew came up behind her, quietly advising her about something. She shook her head and they shrugged and walked away.

Annie snapped her fingers and pointed at me without looking up. "Navigator Fred. Care to do a navigate?" She looked at Amelia before I had the chance to answer. "Is he any good?"

Amelia responded without hesitation. "The best."

I wasn't sure about that, but I went to Annie's side. The map was crude, but decent enough. One location toward the northeast of the island was marked with an X, and Annie jabbed her finger at it. "I need to get there. Soon."

Soon? I shared a confused glance with Amelia. Admittedly, I wasn't the expert here, but I was fairly confident buried treasure didn't go bad. "You don't have a navigator?"

"Rexy didn't trust him. Didn't have time to find a new one, but luckily we found you."

Every time she mentioned Rexy, I wanted to meet them less. "Lucky," I repeated, running my hands through my hair. "Right, how do days work here?"

Annie squinted at me, tilting her head slightly. "Elaborate."

"Fred's trying to work out directions based on the position of the sun," Amelia explained.

"Exactly. You said the magnetic field isn't like back home, I'm trying to figure out what else is different. How many hours in a day? Where does the sun rise?"

"Oh, that. Close enough to Earth days, and in the east." Annie crossed her arms, and for the first time she looked uncertain. "Can you get me there before sunset?"

"Why sunset?" Amelia asked.

"Simple explanation—"

At the sound of rustling in the undergrowth, Annie held up her fist, signaling for us to stop. After a moment, a small reptile darted in front of us and disappeared into the forest, and we continued on.

The island didn't have a large enough ecosystem to support any dinosaurs of intimidating size, thankfully, but we had been seeing little guys like that all day. And all day, Annie hadn't been bothering to stop for them.

She seemed quite content pretending this one might have been a threat, if it would let her avoid Amelia's question.

"You were saying?" I prompted, figuring at the very least we deserved to know what we were about to walk into.

Annie narrowed her eyes but kept staring straight ahead, clearing foliage from our path with her hand and sword. "Time-sensitive treasure."

"What does that mean?" Amelia asked, and I glanced at the crew behind us in case they thought we were causing trouble and wanted to respond in kind.

Annie ignored the question, and an uneasy feeling started twisting in my gut. Amelia's, too, judging by her expression.

"Now, listen," Amelia said, gentle but with no room for nonsense in her voice. "I understand we aren't in any place to make demands, and I appreciate you being more accommodating than most pirates. But if you want our help, I think Fred and I deserve a little open communication about what you're doing here."

It took Annie so long to respond, I had started to give up hope that she would. She just stared into the jungle, eyes distant, taking out some unknown but intense emotion on the plants that dared stand in her way.

Finally, "There was a girl. Mary."

Annie only spoke loud enough for myself and Amelia to hear. Not like it was a secret so much as something revered, holy. Her words were a prayer and the jungle, her cathedral.

"Neither of us wanted to belong to anyone else, but she was mine and I was hers and now she's dead. They all are, victims of Englishmen who try so hard to control something that they end up destroying it." She kicked a rock out of her way with more force than necessary. "I got out, thanks to some glorious nobody undoubtedly already forgotten by history, but the wormhole closed before Mary could join me. My contact says another is due to open here tonight, sunset."

"Mary will meet us, then?" I asked.

Another long silence. "When the next wormhole opens in Spanish Town, Mary's already dead."

I didn't understand. "Then what—"

"Our baby."

It could have been simple. Should have been.

The portal would open, connecting Earth with this prehistoric purgatory, and Annie's contact would bring the baby that had been born while Mary awaited her execution. If Annie didn't show before the portal closed—apparently a bit less than twenty minutes later, though I didn't ask how they calculated this and can't speak to the accuracy—the child would disappear into history, raised as a happily insignificant nobody.

But the sky had turned to flames of sunset that now smoldered at the edges of charcoal night, and still no sign of the portal.

Annie waited on the edge of the clearing, light from the campfire playing dramatically on her face. I had only just met her, but somehow I knew she would send the rest of us away and wait here forever if it came down to that.

"Who's the father?" I asked, sitting beside her.

"Isn't one," Annie answered automatically, staring straight ahead as she carved chunks out of a branch with a knife borrowed from one of her crew. "If you're asking who made the pregnancy possible, that'd be my favorite disaster Jack Rackham, but make no mistake, Mary and I are the parents of that baby."

At that moment, it happened. Everything happened.

And it should have been simple.

A figure appeared on the other side of the clearing carrying something in their arms, the darkness of evening unsteady behind them. I looked at Amelia; we had better lighting the morning of our disappearance, but it was the same shimmering anomaly we had flown through in the Electra.

Sobbing and laughing at the same time, Annie dropped the knife and branch, halfway to the figure before the items hit the ground. She held out her arms, desperately reaching to take the bundle of blankets.

The other person came out of nowhere, taking the baby in the same motion they dropped the person holding them. One of Annie's crew, one of her trusted nobodies, now held her baby for ransom, her contact bleeding but still breathing at their feet.

Annie didn't hesitate, not for a second. Her hand went to her back, reaching for a knife that wasn't there, that's why she'd had to borrow one. Amelia tapped my arm, pointed at the rest of the crew.

Could we trust any of them? Not as much as we could trust each other. Amelia went to Annie's side, standing by to support or potentially restrain the captain if her profanity-laden threats gave way to actions that could put the child at risk of harm.

In reality, it didn't much matter what people thought Amelia was up to, so long as they thought about her instead of me.

If anyone noticed me picking up the knife from beside the campfire, they made no attempt to stop me as I made my way around the clearing and positioned myself off to the side and slightly behind the mutineer demanding ransom.

I didn't kill the person. Even if the idea of taking a life didn't bother me, I wasn't about to deprive Rexy the pleasure. But I spilled blood before they even knew I was there, and delivered the baby to Annie.

"It would be home," Amelia said, and I couldn't tell whether she was trying to convince me or herself.

"It would be 1721," I reminded her.

She put her hands on her hips, scrutinizing the portal. Some creature screeched in the distance. "No dinosaurs in 1721."

Tempting. "No airplanes in 1721."

This gave her pause. I couldn't imagine Amelia Earhart without airplanes. I'm not sure she could either.

"We could become pirates." She wasn't serious, but she wasn't entirely joking.

"Golden age of piracy is almost over," I pointed out, because if we stalled long enough talking about it, the decision would make itself.

Amelia pursed her lips in thought, tilting her head to the side. "We could stay here a while. Maybe find a way home one day."

I gave a nod. "We could become pirates."

We stood there a moment longer before turning to look at Annie beaming at her baby like they were the most precious treasure any pirate could ever dream of. Mary Frederick, she named them, "Or Mark Frederica, whatever they decide."

Amelia nudged me with her elbow, grinning. "Bet Harry Manning never did anything like this."

A Connecticut Yangchuanosaurus in King Arthur's Court

All right, I gotta be honest. When my chute didn't open, I thought I was a dead man.

So I made the sign of the cross and said a little prayer asking for forgiveness—never been a religious man, but I figured, what have I got to lose?—and I closed my eyes. I don't know why. Just didn't find the idea of watching the ground come up to meet me very appealing, I guess.

I hit the trees almost immediately. Way too soon, factoring in my speed and the elevation of the plane, but I wouldn't realize that for a while. Having branches scratching and beating every part of your body, the constant cacophony of thrashing leaves in your ears, that ain't exactly conducive to complicated mental mathematics.

The noisy assault ended as abruptly as it started, one last branch grabbing my malfunctioning chute. Sharp pain bloomed at my chest and groin as the straps dug instant bruises into my body.

"Goddamn momentum," I wheezed. Hitting the ground probably would've been the less painful option.

I gave myself a minute to catch my breath, and examined my surroundings. Something wasn't right. Something other than me dangling ten feet above the ground like a damn piñata.

It wasn't raining anymore. I touched the nearest leaf: completely dry, and there wasn't any of that rainy dirt smell, what do they call it, petrichor.

How in the hell was I soaking wet from falling through a rainstorm that hadn't even reached the ground?

Trees didn't look right, either. Now admittedly, I'm from the east coast, but I spent a fair amount of time in Oregon before I got on that plane, and even at night I could tell that this was no Oregon. More like a forest of weird palm trees with the occasional oak like the one that grabbed me, and—

I looked up. The last full moon was weeks ago. I shouldn't have been looking at a full moon, and . . . and why didn't the stars look right, why didn't I recognize the constellations?

Panic set in. Full-on, flailing and shouting panic, tugging at the straps and pounding my fist against the tree. I only stopped when I heard heavy, rasping breathing behind me, and my self-preservation instinct took over.

Cautious, thundering footsteps preceded the creature as it walked around the tree.

Creature. Sure, that's one word for it.

It was a dinosaur. A freaking *dinosaur*. Some sort of weird tyrannosaurus-looking bastard, with a massive head at just the right height to look me in the eye.

For the second time in—god, was it only a few minutes?—I was sure I was about to die. Maybe I already had. Maybe this was hell.

Either way, I wasn't going down without a fight. I kicked, only made the slightest contact with the thing's snout. It growled, snapped at me. Not with any real intention, though, like it was just making a point.

"Are you boys done proving you're both alpha males?"

The dinosaur turned to look over his shoulder, and that was the first I noticed the woman standing there. Gorgeous woman, my age or a little younger, dressed like Maid Marian for some reason, her hands on her hips.

"You . . ." My voice failed me briefly. "You, you know this dinosaur, ma'am?"

Her melodious laugh would have been the most beautiful thing I'd ever heard, if it wasn't coming at my expense. "Yes, I know him quite well, which is why I'd rather you stop kicking him. He doesn't like it, and he's liable to leave you hanging there instead of rescuing you."

"Rescue me," I said to myself. "I'm supposed to believe a T. rex is gonna rescue me...."

"Kirby is not a tyrannosaurus, he is a yangchuanosaurus."

Before I could even begin to make sense of what she'd just said, she whistled sharply and the dinosaur turned back to me. In one swift movement, he raised a massive claw and swiped at me, neatly slicing through the straps of the parachute.

Finally, all this time after jumping from the plane, I hit the ground.

"A little warning next time would be nice," I grumbled.

It was ... a lot to take in. And you want to know the real messed up thing? The dinosaurs weren't even the weirdest part.

Aldith, the gal in the Maid Marian getup, lived in a ye olde town straight out of some sort of Knights of the Round Table movie. Lords and ladies, everyone talking British with their thees and thous, even an honest-to-god castle in the middle of that prehistoric jungle.

And they weren't playing around. Said their ancestors came through some magic doorway to this land of dragons. Which they tamed and rode like horses.

Just imagine the ridiculousness of a grown-ass man dressed up like Lancelot, riding this ... deinony-whatever Allie called it. Big lizard-bird nightmare monster with giant disemboweling blades on its feet. Picture that, will ya? And now imagine everyone around you thinks you're the weirdo for thinking it ain't normal.

That's what I was dealing with in this town.

"Camelot, eh?" I asked when we arrived at the gates that first night.

"Camelops," Allie corrected, grinning. I didn't get the joke, but I didn't question it. I already had the feeling my time here would go much smoother if I didn't stop to question every little thing that didn't make sense.

Why supposedly medieval knights had some pretty modern-looking armor, for instance, or why we could understand each other for the most part despite Old English being, to the best of my recollection from school, a lot of nonsense masquerading as a language.

So I minded my business best I could. Tried to, anyway. That lasted about a day and a half.

Look, I ain't claiming to be no genius. If I was, the whole hijacking an airplane thing probably would have gone a lot smoother. But here's the thing, my world was centuries ahead of these guys in terms of technology, and even if I didn't understand exactly how it all worked, I had knowledge they couldn't even dream of.

So I started helping out, doing what I could to remedy little issues around town. Fixed a couple leaks, taught their doctors the basics of germs and handwashing, updated the design of the harnesses on their carts so they could be pulled more efficiently by the para … parasol … I don't know, some big dinosaur with a tube coming outta its head.

And now here's a fun bit of information for you: corrupt political leaders who hide information and purposely keep their citizens living in substandard conditions? Turns out they don't appreciate people coming in and improving things. Who knew.

Truth be told, when I got on that plane I was pretty sure I'd end up dead or in jail. Didn't really expect a medieval dungeon in a world where people ride freaking dinosaurs, but in the grand scheme of things, I wasn't too far off.

Never thought there'd be a beautiful lady coming to visit me, though.

In my brief time spent with the townsfolk, I got the impression they didn't take in a lot of outsiders. Allie rescuing me and bringing me in, I think in her mind, that made me her responsibility.

"I really wish you'd stop associating yourself with me," I lied when the guards let her in on the morning of my third day. Okay, half-lied. I meant it, I just also hoped she would ignore me. That woman was a bright spot in a very dimly lit cave, and I can't deny that the food she brought made me seriously consider falling in love with her a little bit.

"No such luck," Allie informed me, passing a plate of scrambled eggs and toast through the bars. "At least, not if you want my help getting you out of here," she added, petting the cat-sized dinosaur curled in the crook of her arm.

Damn woman looked so out of place, dressed up like a princess—no, she was a decade or two too beautiful, make that a queen—complete with the pointy hat and veil, surrounded by jail cells dug into the cave walls and filled with criminals and filth. But it didn't faze her in the least. I had to chuckle.

She frowned. "And what, may I ask, is so funny?"

I just shook my head, poked at the eggs she brought. "Is there any chance these aren't dinosaur eggs? You got any chickens hidden away on a farm somewhere?"

"Even if we did, they would still be dinosaur eggs, Mr. Cooper. Birds are dinosaurs. That's how evolution works."

Now like I said, I'm not the brightest tool in the shed. Worked at my dad's paint and tile store instead of going to school most days. But even I knew there wasn't no way these Renaissance folk had any idea about evolution. They probably still believed you could change lead into gold and—

Wait.

Crossing my arms, I leaned closer to the bars. "I hear you right? You wanna bust me out of here?"

"You don't sound particularly enthused by the idea," Allie pointed out. "And I can't help but notice that with all the questions you asked about Avalonia after Kirby and I rescued you, not once did you mention wanting to go home."

I conceded this point with a raise of my eyebrows, and picked at the eggs while thinking of a response. They looked enough like chicken eggs, and I decided to pretend they were.

"Fate is kinda like those diner-nonner things you guys ride," I said finally.

"Deinonychus," Allie corrected.

"Yeah, that's exactly what I just said."

She smiled and shook her head. "You can just call them raptors."

"All right. Fate is like a raptor. You can run from it all you want, but it's smarter than you and it's faster than you, and just when you think it's safe to stop running, it's already there waiting for you."

For a long moment, the only sounds were the grumbling of the other prisoners and my fork scraping against my plate.

"Fate wanted you to come here?" Allie asked.

I shook my head. "Nah. Fate wanted to punish me."

I didn't elaborate, she didn't ask me to. Just stood there, thinking and petting the dinosaur while I kept pretending I was eating chicken eggs.

"My motives for freeing you aren't entirely altruistic," she admitted finally. "Living under the king's rule means living in a dictatorship built on theocracy, misogyny, hatred of science…." She paused here, like maybe she had never said it out loud before. "Fate brought me here as well. I have an idea, a way to replace him and start improving the way we live."

A couple yards away and well within hearing range, the guards made a big show of ignoring our conversation. Whatever she was about to say, seemed like they were in favor of it.

"I need someone like you," Allie told me, the fire from the torch lights blazing in the reflection of her eyes.

"Why me?"

"Because you aren't from the middle ages."

"Yeah, and neither are you." When she opened her mouth to protest, I added, "If you were, I'm pretty sure you wouldn't be calling it the middle ages. You'd be calling it…" I waved a hand vaguely. "Whatever they called it back then. 'Ye olde nowadays' or something."

A pleased smile on her face, Allie stepped closer, hooking her arms around the bars of my cell so she could put her weight on the door. "See, I knew you were clever. Just the kind of man I need to fix things around here."

The history books—whenever this place gets over its fear of literacy long enough to develop the printing press—they'll say I was the mastermind. And they'll be wrong.

Nah. I'll take the credit to keep the blame off her, but it was all Allie. Brilliant woman, absolutely brilliant.

She claimed to be a scientist in her time, decades after I jumped out of that plane in '71. It was a lie, neither of us pretended otherwise, but it's not like D.B. Cooper was my real name. If it mattered, she would tell me eventually.

In any event, she figured out the pattern of when portals opened between our world and this one. She tried explaining it to me, wrote out long and complicated formulas in chalk on the walls of the dungeon. I pretended to follow along, and she pretended to believe me for a couple minutes before laughing and shaking her head.

"Just memorize your lines, Mr. Cooper," she said with a fond roll of her eyes.

"That, I can do."

"You heard me," I all but shouted, slamming my hand into the iron bars. "I said it real clear, what part didn't you understand? The part where I'm a wizard, or the part where I'm a wizard?"

The man, some squire or whatever sent from the castle to check the validity of my claims, hesitated.

"Well?"

"I understood thine words," he assured me slowly, "it's merely...if thou truly were endowed with powers from beyond our realm, why hast thou not used them to free thyself from these confines until present?"

"'Cause this dungeon serves the best scrambled eggs I've ever had," I deadpanned, and the irritated look on his face told me they most certainly had sarcasm in whatever ye olde time this mook came from. "Look," I said, leveling with him. "I've been trying to think of a spell that'll get me out of here without destroying your entire village, but I can't, and I'm getting bored of listenin' to the bard in the next cell sing about dinosaurs I can't pronounce."

That part, not a lie. I'd be willing to bet he was imprisoned for the crime of subjecting people to his voice.

"You don't believe me."

Of course he didn't. Maybe the townsfolk believed the fantasy told by the big man on the throne, but anyone from the castle, according to Allie, they knew the truth. Wasn't no magic in the world, just science and liars.

"Let me prove it to you," I offered. "Tomorrow, right about noon, I'm gonna create a second sun in the sky."

He chuckled.

"You won't be laughing tomorrow, buddy." I put my face up to the bars, narrowing my eyes. "You tell that king of yours, if I ain't freed within ten minutes of that second sun appearing in the sky, I'll drop it. Right on the castle. Flatten everyone inside. And then I'll burn this place to the ground on my way out of here."

If I didn't know better, I'd say a little bit of fear, a little bit of doubt, flashed across his face before he rolled his eyes and went to pass on my message.

I waited the whole next morning, my stomach knotted up worse than it'd been before I got on the plane in Portland.

God, what a wild couple of days. Going from skyjacker to possible co-savior of an entire people....

For the longest time, nothing. Had to be close to noon, maybe even past. Was Allie wrong about the portal? Or did someone finally give up the ruse and admit there was no such thing as magic, just to discredit my claims?

And then the screaming started. I could hear it all the way down in the dungeons, the sound of people losing their shit on account of no one letting them understand the natural—weird as all hell, but natural—phenomena of the world around them.

Granted, even with Allie's attempts at explaining it to me, I'm pretty sure I'd be shrieking right along with them, if a portal to another time opened up at just the right angle to make it look like the sun had doubled itself.

Luckily, I didn't see it, leaving me to be the poster boy for calm and smug wizards when everyone stormed the dungeon, demanding I put out the second sun. Allie was among the group, smiling brighter than any amount of suns.

I winked at her. Still didn't quite understand exactly how she planned to do this, but we'd just completed step one of bringing her society to a more advanced age of enlightenment, and it seemed like a hell of a lot more fun than going back home.

Tinker Tailor Soldier Spinosaurus

When someone received the honor of being knighted, there was ceremony. Pageantry. Music and outfits and speeches, no expense spared to drive home the point that this was more than a job, this was a calling, something that could only be bestowed on the most exemplary candidates.

There was no such ceremony when Enid of Camelops was stripped of her knighthood. She was merely informed that she was to turn in her sword and armor at the blacksmith to be melted down.

They could have her armor; it held no particular place in her heart. It was just a symbol of her kingdom's most skilled metal-workers keeping her safe while trusting her to keep them safe, merely the uniform she put on every morning that fit every curve of her body like a second skin.

So maybe it had a place in her heart. They could still have it.

But they could not have her sword. She had earned and regretted every drop of blood spilled by that blade, her own and others'. It was part of her. They could take her title, her honor, but they could not take her sword.

Not knowing exactly how one was meant to dispose of a sword they were no longer allowed to own, Enid did the most sensible thing she could think of.

She chucked it into a lake.

Swords, lakes, it matched the vibe of her knockoff Medieval Times kingdom that she had loved with her entire heart until that morning. And anyway, it was satisfying, watching the ripples disperse and knowing it was gone from her life but still there if she needed it.

She sat on the shore, her chin resting in her hands, and watched the sails of distant spinosaurs drifting through the water.

That's all they were. Spinosaurs. Magnificent animals, but just animals, not the dragons the coat of arms made them out to be.

What had she done wrong? She couldn't think of anything remotely interesting that had occurred over the past few days, just ordinary patrol, raptor jousting in the evenings, no word of impending attack by dinosaur or rival humans. Really, she hadn't been given the opportunity to do anything wrong.

Unless. . . .

Enid threw a rock in the lake, channeling all of her rage into making as big a splash as possible.

Things had been better since the self-proclaimed wizard had assumed power; he and his queen didn't seem to tolerate the hatred encouraged by their predecessors. But they could only do so much if they wanted their subjects to remain loyal. Too much change too quickly might lead to a coup, and one of those a year was really more than enough.

But maybe another coup was just what they needed.

For a long while, Enid drifted away into thoughts of everything and nothing, of what used to be and what could've been. The real world faded, growing blurry, but snapped into focus the instant she heard a twig breaking behind her.

She moved on instinct, rising to her feet and spinning around slowly enough that her movement wouldn't startle a predator. Her hand went to her belt, grasping at the memory of her sword.

Before her stood a figure in a dark hooded cloak. Tall, on the feminine side if Enid had to guess. She wore sunglasses, the big kind like Jackie Kennedy used to wear back in what Enid used to call the real world, and her skin was quite a few shades lighter than Enid's.

"State your business," Enid demanded, hoping the tears on her cheeks wouldn't distract from her authoritative appearance.

The woman didn't seem to care one way or the other, just gave a smile so mysterious she must've practiced in a mirror and said, "If you want to make a difference, I have a job for you."

"She wants you to do what?"

"Everything will be fine," Enid assured her girlfriend as she went around their small cottage, gathering up belongings in an old sack. "I've gone undercover before, there's no active battleground the way I'm going, and maybe things will get a little better for people around here soon."

Erica shook her head in disbelief. "Yes, I get that. Very noble of you, as always. It's just the details I'm a little hazy on."

Enid made a vague noise and stopped to consider her wardrobe. Exactly how many outfits should one bring when defecting to a rival land?

"You're also hazy on the details, aren't you?" Though Erica sounded annoyed, almost angry, she still walked over to their shared wardrobe and started shoving things in the bag. "Just pants and shirts, I'm not sure they dress up over there."

"Thank you," Enid said brightly, using one of the shirts to wrap a small dagger she wanted to bring for safety.

"Are you even paying attention to me, babe?"

This finally snapped Enid out of whatever fog had taken over her brain. She dropped the bag, turned and placed one hand on either side of Erica's face, and kissed her.

The kiss wasn't deep or passionate, but then neither was Enid. It was just full of love, devotion, the way she would kiss Erica in matching wedding dresses in front of the entire kingdom if it was allowed.

"Yes," she whispered, breaking the kiss but keeping their foreheads pressed together as she stroked Erica's blonde curls. "I am always paying attention to you. All of this is for you. For us."

"You don't even know what you're doing." Erica tried to sound like she was scolding, but she just sounded scared.

"I am . . . trying to make a difference. Trying to end this war, even if it means we lose." Enid reconsidered. "Maybe especially if it means we lose. The details don't change my mind."

Erica wiped her eyes, tried to laugh. "Well, you better succeed in whatever this is. Camelops will charge you with treason if you don't."

Enid kissed her girlfriend who should have been her wife. "At least treason actually is a crime."

A different contact met Enid at the lake. A man, lanky and kind of crooked, his face covered with a scarf that matched his camouflage cloak. When he handed her the books, Enid thought she saw a flash of familiar maroon and gold under his sleeve, but didn't mention it.

"Any questions?" he asked.

Too many. Enid suspected he wouldn't answer most of them.

"Will anyone get hurt if I do this?"

The man hesitated a moment, considering his answer. "It's war, milady. People get hurt either way. Maybe this time, they'll be the last."

He gave a small bow, as if she still merited the respect given to a knight, and all but disappeared into the forest.

Enid held the books to her chest. Three volumes, each about two inches thick. They were handbound in leather, and by the feel of it, not the cheap stuff Erica used as trim on the clothing she made.

She could read them. Probably should read them, see what exactly she was smuggling into enemy territory.

Looking back at the spires of the castle looming over all those good people just trying to make it through life without trouble, however, Enid had to rephrase that thought. She could read the books and see what exactly she was smuggling *out of* enemy territory.

What if it was something she didn't agree with? As long as she didn't look, she wouldn't know, she could get out and get Erica out and nothing else mattered.

It wouldn't be accurate to say Enid turned her back on the kingdom and walked away without a second thought. There were second thoughts, and thirds, even fourths. They bounced around inside her head, anxiety and fear reverberating against her skull with every step.

She just didn't let them stop her.

It should have been simple.

Go to New Hell Creek, meet her contact in the library, and convince them she wanted to defect. Which wouldn't be that difficult, as Enid had decided she truly did want that.

But nothing was ever as simple as it should have been. Enid had learned that long ago.

The town lacked any towering castles that could be seen from afar, but the wild prehistoric landscape showed signs of human influence as she got closer. A swath of tree stumps where part of the forest had been sacrificed for lumber, a water wheel happily turning in a sparkling creek, fields of something that was not quite wheat and some animals that were not quite cows.

Enid took her time, her path meandering and her pace unhurried. She stopped to consider the animals that were not quite cows, aurochs maybe, or a relative, and used the opportunity to examine the woodworking of the fence and iron hinges of the gate. She learned two important things:

The people of New Hell Creek were more technologically advanced than she had been told, equal to or possibly surpassing Camelops.

And she was most certainly being followed.

She hadn't seen anyone, only heard them, more distantly now that there was less cover but absolutely following her. Again she longed for her sword, for the safety and authority of her armor; she didn't dare confront anyone without them.

Enid continued on, and the fields became farmland became the outskirts of town. They had sentry towers, guards, but no real wall, no border between "them" and "us."

At first glance, New Hell Creek seemed as if it would be relatively easy to conquer, which must have made it all the more infuriating for the king. But Enid had seen their armies in action. Small but scrappy, like a pack of compsognathus, with swords and arrows and, according to occasional reports, some sort of blasting magic implement.

Pistols, Enid realized as a guard approached her and she caught a glimpse of his holster beneath his long jacket. She hadn't lived in the timeline proper since she was in elementary school, nearly three decades now, but she remembered cowboy movies, at least vaguely.

And a vague memory of cowboy movies seemed to be the vibe here.

"State your business?" the guard asked politely, tipping his Stetson in a gesture reminiscent of Camelops knights raising the visor of their helmets.

"Enid Harriet," Enid said, catching the "milord" just before it left her mouth. "I have books for the library."

This caught his attention. "Books?"

"Three volumes of *Raptors in the Long Grass*."

The guard gave a small nod at the code phrase and waved her in. "Welcome to New Hell Creek."

"Different than you expected?"

Enid nodded slowly, stepping away from her contact to wander down the rows of bookshelves that took up the majority of the cramped but cozy library. The selection of reading material was like the town itself, everything from hand-bound classics and lovingly dog-eared religious texts to scientific textbooks and bodice rippers in bright dust jackets, things that didn't seem to go together but still somehow worked.

"Why do we hate you?" Enid marveled.

"Pardon?"

Enid turned to face her contact, a pleasant man introduced only as Crater, and shrugged. "Everyone is friendly, welcoming. You have books here we would burn as sacrilege. You have—" She felt her voice threatening to break and simply gestured at the rainbow banner billowing gently outside the window. "Why are we told to hate you?"

"A very good question," Crater said with a sigh. He wasn't much older than Enid, forties perhaps, but carried himself with the distinguished weariness of someone far more advanced in age.

Then again, perhaps it was the way he dressed that gave him that air. Crisp white shirt with a gray vest and trousers, impossibly dainty glasses, and a twirly little mustache, like the owner of a general store in the Old West.

"A good story properly told," Crater said, almost addressing the books more than Enid, "is capable of inspiring people to do almost anything. A good story improperly told, even more powerful." He gestured at a small sitting area and kitchen attached to the library. "Coffee or tea?"

"Coffee," Enid guessed. They didn't have either in Camelops.

"There is much I can't tell you yet," Crater said, busying himself at the woodstove. "And even more I may never be able to tell you. But suffice it to say your kingdom wanted a resource in our territory, we didn't believe they should have it, and they have gone to great lengths to ensure that every child in Camelops grows up hating us and everything we believe in."

Enid sat in one of the two plush armchairs ensconcing a wooden end table scattered with mechanical parts and projects in various stages of completion. One appeared to be a small camera, assembled with the slightly crude precision of a child trying their best, complete with copper plates that could fit in a pocket.

They had cameras in Camelops, but such technology was strictly controlled as the ruling class desperately clung to the notion that progress meant the destruction of the ideals the kingdom was built on. Enid pulled her bag into her lap. Her hand slipped inside and found embroidery on the interior. "E+E" in rainbow thread, an anniversary present she didn't dare show off.

"These books will help you win the war?"

"That is the hope, yes."

"And if you win? Oh, thank you." Enid took the offered mug and sniffed it. The coffee didn't smell bad, per se, it just smelled a lot, and she couldn't decide how she felt about it. "What will happen if you win the war? What changes will you bring to Camelops?"

Crater gave her a small smile as he relaxed into the chair beside her. "And I thought *I* was evaluating *your* trustworthiness. Don't apologize," he said, holding up a finger. "I like this. Shows initiative."

Enid sipped her coffee. It smelled more soothing than it tasted, but not bad.

"If New Hell Creek should reign victorious, Miss Harriet, your people would be free. Kings and queens replaced by elected officials, a justice system operating in daylight rather than shadows, and, if I may be so bold as to make an assumption, you would be able to marry the woman you love."

Another sip of coffee, trying to mask the sudden wave of emotions. "Erica," Enid said when she had composed herself.

Crater gave her a smile as warm as the coffee and not nearly as bitter. "You would be able to marry Erica. In the town square, if you like."

Enid knew she should probably think this over, consider the risks of trusting this man, this town. For all she knew, this was all some big manipulation to get her on his side.

But she was tired of not being married to Erica, of not being able to kiss her wherever she liked and hold her hand and say the words "my wife."

Erica was worth the risk. Erica was worth every risk.

"I was followed here."

The suddenness of this statement seemed to surprise Crater, but he nodded grimly. "Yes, I was worried you might be. Finish your coffee. This will be a bit more complicated than I had hoped."

Enid had been loyal to Camelops, not as a choice so much as by default. It was her home, she loved it, and by the time she was old enough to realize it didn't love her back, it had been drilled into her head that she had no other options.

The kingdom was decent to her. It paid enough to keep her and Erica comfortable and until recently looked the other way when it came to just how comfortable they were together, and for that she proudly wore its colors and defended its borders.

Her loyalty now lay at the bottom of the lake. She threw it away as easily as Camelops threw her away. It stung, deep in her heart, but she should have done it sooner and couldn't imagine actively making the choice to give the kingdom her loyalty.

Someone else did not have that problem.

According to Crater—Enid had no reason to trust him, but she had no reason to trust Camelops either, and she felt safer with him—the New Hell Creek agent working from within the kingdom had been sabotaged several times already in their attempt to smuggle the books out. If Camelops had followed Enid, she and the library would be in danger.

The conversation about what to do next was put on pause when Crater's daughter came home from school. Energetic little thing, just this side of too young to disillusion and frighten with talk of war and espionage but old enough to give herself a code name like her father. Star.

Enid already had enough personal reasons to continue with this mission, but it became all the more real somehow when she met Star. New Hell Creek needed to win this war, she couldn't let that little girl grow up under Camelops rule.

She caught Crater on his way to the kitchen in the morning, launching into the discussion again as if the previous twelve-hour interruption hadn't happened.

"They may not know I was smuggling books, or even who I am, only that someone has defected here with information. I think we should try to find them before they find us, identify who they are and—" She interrupted herself. "Do you know if there is any truth to the rumors of a savior?"

Crater gave her a tired but amused smile. "Been reading?"

"All night."

"And how many more cups of coffee did you have after I retired?"

Enid frowned in confusion. "Why?"

"Later I shall direct you to the encyclopedia entry on caffeine." Crater rolled up his sleeves, began preparing breakfast. "We should not rely on the savior. His is yet another good story properly told, something to give our children hope."

Enid said nothing for a moment, hiding her disappointment by tidying the makeshift bed in the sitting area she hadn't used the night before. It had felt nice, letting herself believe someone was coming to save everyone.

"What can I do?" she asked, emptying her bag and proudly turning it inside out so Erica's handiwork could be displayed.

Crater gave her a nod of approval before going back to mixing something that looked like pancake batter. "You can go rouse my daughter, if the smell of breakfast doesn't do it first."

"I meant. . . ." Enid gestured at the books, at herself, at the vague direction of the entire universe as she went down the hall to Star's bedroom.

"Yes, that. Our mystery friend will be searching for you, I thought perhaps you might make yourself easy to find and hope they reveal themselves in some way."

Enid knocked on the door, opening it when there was no response. She covered her mouth in shock.

It seemed their mystery friend had already found her. Star was gone.

"This is my fault, I brought them here," Enid apologized again, frantically trying to calm herself, to remember the detached composure of a knight.

"The only person to blame is the person who took her." Crater had no obligation to show her such grace, but he remained the gentleman as they searched the library and yard for evidence, even as more and more panic encroached on his face. He ran his hands through his hair, deep breaths steadying the quaver in his voice. "But why take her, why not just the books?"

"Threatening us so we won't try this again," Enid said, the words "us" and "we" coming with surprising ease. She started to say something else, stopped herself.

Some of the little projects on the end table were gone, including the camera.

Wordlessly, Enid went to her bag and pulled out the three books. "They didn't take the books?" Crater asked.

"They didn't take your daughter, either," Enid said, unsure if this development made things easier or harder. "She's smart?"

"Unquestionably brilliant."

Enid nodded to herself. "She figured out what's going on. She's trying to find the spy herself."

The steeds ridden in New Hell Creek were more stocky and lacked the finesse of the ones from the royal stables. A different species of raptor, or perhaps bred for different qualities.

But they were intuitive. At least, Enid's borrowed steed was. Kelly, charcoal gray with a lighter underbelly and streaks of purple in her wing feathers, responded to subtle movements as Enid shifted her weight in the saddle, turning or stopping without a single verbal command.

One less thing to worry about as they moved through the sparse woods just outside town. With any luck, the girl hadn't gone far and her father would find her roaming the streets with a magnifying glass, but if Star thought the enemy spy had a hideout in the woods, she may have gone out there.

Enid and Kelly made several circuits of the town, expanding the search each time. Crater sent another operative to Camelops just in case she had been taken, but otherwise informed no one.

"On the off-chance our mystery friend does have her," he had explained, "I have to assume we might have a double agent. The man I sent back to your kingdom, I trust with my life and my heart and that includes my daughter. And you.... Well, quite honestly, I believe you are trustworthy but I don't trust you much at all yet. There is no value in you being a double agent."

As if anyone in Camelops valued her enough to make her a spy.

Erica, she supposed, but the opinion of a plain, simple tailor unfortunately made little difference in the minds of those in charge.

A mechanical sound cut through the early morning tranquility, not overly loud but harsh and artificial. In a calming gesture, Enid put her hand on the back of Kelly's neck as the raptor became perfectly still.

Enid listened, her eyes searching the overlapping optical illusions made by the foliage. Kelly tilted her head to the side, curiously sniffing the air with her lips curled back to show her teeth.

Camera shutter, Enid realized when they heard it a second time, and urged her raptor to follow the sound. Cooling relief washed through Enid's body when they came upon Star, unharmed and still in her pajamas, taking photographs of an indentation in the grass where it appeared someone had spent the night.

"Star," Enid hissed.

The child looked up, smiling sheepishly. "Hi."

"Shh. Come here, we need to go home."

"I was just trying to help. I found—"

"I know. Thank you. I'm taking you home."

The raptor's head swung sharply to the left, her body tense and her eyes predatory. Enid put her hand on the hilt of the borrowed sword at her belt. It didn't feel right but it would do.

"Get on," she told Star, holding the reins tightly for the first time. She didn't know what the raptor heard, but the crest of head feathers raising defensively was enough. She had to get the kid home.

The instant Star scrambled up and wrapped her arms around Enid, they turned and sprinted back toward New Hell Creek.

They were being followed. Multiple riders, but Enid resisted the urge to look back and count, lest Star realize the danger of the situation.

But of course she already had. The kid was smarter than anyone gave her credit for.

"Who are they?" she asked in a small voice.

"Knights of Camelops," Enid answered.

"How can you tell?"

A fallen tree lay directly in front of them. Enid leaned to the left. The raptor turned at the suggestion but made a disgruntled chirp as if she had been planning to jump it.

"I saw the armor."

"What about the blonde lady?"

"What blonde lady?"

Star's arms shifted around Enid as if in a shrug. "It was her sleeping spot I took pictures of. She isn't with the others. She had a bag, kind of like yours—"

Erica. How, why, Enid didn't know or care. It was Erica.

They had to be close to the edge of the woods, almost back to New Hell Creek and an army that could outnumber the handful of knights behind them. Almost home.

Enid slowed her raptor. "Which way did she go?" When Star didn't answer, she added, "You aren't in trouble for spying, which way did she go?"

"Toward the river."

"Hold on tight," Enid said, stopping Kelly entirely and turning to face the oncoming soldiers.

Star did as requested. "Why?"

Enid waited until the distant sounds of raptors became distant visuals, making sure they could see her.

"We're gonna lose them."

With that, she urged Kelly into a run, charging toward the enemies for a few dozen yards and then cutting sharply to the side, crashing through the thickest foliage and disappearing.

The raptors of Camelops went through rigorous training. They were skilled, obedient, deadly.

But they trained on easy terrain. Flat grassland, wide trails. A Camelops raptor would never consider jumping over a fallen tree, not without significant convincing from the rider.

Enid pointed Kelly in the right direction and then trusted her to make it through the tight and twisting corridors between trees, ducking and holding on to the raptor's neck as low branches slashed just inches from their heads.

They ran parallel to the knights, forcing them to stop and turn abruptly before trying to follow. Enid could hear them falling behind and made a sharp course correction that put more distance between them.

When she thought they were far enough ahead, Enid signaled for Kelly to stop. She pointed at a sprawling oak tree.

"Climb up there," she whispered to Star. "Be quiet, no pictures. Wait for me."

"But I—"

Enid turned to look behind her, putting her hand on Star's

shoulder. "I know you want to help. You've done a great job so far. But now I need you to hide in the tree so I know you're safe, that's how you can help me the most."

Reluctantly, Star dismounted and, after giving the raptor a pat on the hip, climbed the tree.

Enid watched to make sure she was concealed from view before urging Kelly on. They took a winding path, eventually losing the knights altogether before making their way to the river.

And there was Erica, sitting in the grass and smiling like she expected this all along.

Enid still didn't understand, but that could wait. She got down off the raptor and went to kiss the woman she loved more than anyone and anything, a kiss that redefined loyalty and devotion.

"What are you doing here?" Enid asked, whispering against her lips.

"I saw you being followed when you left." Erica pulled back from the embrace just enough to look into Enid's eyes as she touched her cheek. "I did some spying of my own. I came to warn you but the town would see me as less of a threat in daylight, and then the knights—"

"Warn me? About what?"

"I know who asked you to smuggle out the books."

Enid raised her eyebrows, impressed.

"Voices carry in the palace and people talk in front of the help," Erica said with a shrug, but she was clearly proud of herself. "I don't know if we can trust the information in them."

"Who is it?"

"The queen."

For the first time since receiving the books, Enid actually opened them. Erica and Crater read over her shoulder, and Star was already sprawled on the floor with the next volume.

Erica had feared the queen being behind this smuggling operation meant the books would be filled with erroneous information, bad intel meant to sabotage New Hell Creek. Logical fears, but ultimately unfounded.

The first book contained decades of research into the portals connecting Avalonia and Earth, diligently collected data in a dozen different handwritings documenting where and when and for how long the portals opened. Formulas to predict them.

Forbidden technologies made up the second book. Blueprints and diagrams and scientific theories from a time far beyond the one Camelops pretended to be stuck in.

And finally, a personal history of Camelops written by the queen herself. The truth of its origins, the needless war, how she and her king schemed to take over from the previous tyrant.

At the very end, there was a plea for help.

"She wants to lose the war," Enid read aloud, not sure if she was comprehending correctly. "She and the king are trying to change things, but they're just figureheads and they can only do so much. But if Camelops loses the war, New Hell Creek gets to take the real bad guys out of power and replace them with people who care about freedom and human rights."

They all sat in silence for a moment, absorbing this. Enid got up and walked toward the door.

"Where are you going?" Erica asked.

Enid smiled at her. "To get my sword out of the lake, and then I'm coming back here and asking you to marry me while we work on winning this war."

Pterodactyl We Meet Again

Terrible video connection, just terrible. The movements of her mouth didn't match up with her voice at all.

But Josh was reasonably sure she just said "reports of a dinosaur coming through a wormhole."

He scrambled out of his chair to get a notepad, nearly tripping over the model city made from recycled goods his daughter had to build for school. This could be it, the big story that put his name on the front page of every newspaper. Maybe even the online ones.

"Can you repeat that, Doc?" Josh asked, skidding back into frame with a pen and paper.

Dr. Shirakawa repeated herself, more slowly this time, and Josh felt his face growing warm as he wrote down her actual statement. What an embarrassment this almost was, he could just imagine the mockery if he had actually gone to the press saying there were dinosaurs in the modern world.

Pterodactyl. Dr. Shirakawa had said she had reports of a *pterodactyl* coming through a wormhole, and everybody knew pterodactyls weren't actually dinosaurs.

"Reports," Josh said, and wrote the word on his pad, underlining it three times like a professional. The ink was purple glitter, must have grabbed one of Samantha's. "You didn't see this yourself, then?"

She shook her head. "I was in my lab. I heard screaming outside the window, but by the time I looked, I only caught a glimpse of"—Dr. Shirakawa made a wiggling motion with her hand—"in the air. Like asphalt on a hot summer day. Witnesses corroborate this, saying the pterodactyl came through this disturbance."

Josh nibbled thoughtfully on the end of the gel pen, taking in the enormity of what this could mean, not only for the scientific community but, more importantly, for his career. Did they only put sports people on Wheaties boxes, or would they make an exception for a particularly exemplary reporter?

He made another note: "call General Mills."

"So what are we talking in terms of wingspan," Josh asked. "Single engine airplane? Toyota RAV4? Polar bear?"

When there was no response, he looked up to see the doctor frozen in the middle of a strange facial expression.

He pointed to his ear. "Sorry, I can't hear you, I think it's glitching again."

"No, it's working fine," Dr. Shirakawa said, staring at him strangely for another moment. "Maybe a meter at most. Easily mistaken for a bird or flying fox if not for the shape of the face, and people in a nearby village have described similar creatures appearing occasionally over the past few months."

Josh tried to hide his excitement. Play it cool. He leaned back in his chair, maybe playing it a bit too cool, had to grab the desk to keep from falling over. "And you've no doubt read all of my highly acclaimed articles and blog posts theorizing that legendary creatures such as sasquatch and the Loch Ness monster are actually extinct animals who have been transported through time, and contacted me as the preeminent expert in the subject."

The connection froze again briefly so Josh didn't hear Dr. Shirakawa agree with his assessment of himself. Oh well, there would be time for that later, when she was writing a blurb for the bestseller he would inevitably write.

"I appreciate you not hanging up on me yet," she said with a tired chuckle. "This isn't my field of expertise, I study global warming, not . . . temporal anomalies? But if you'll take this seriously, I would love to invite you to visit."

Visit some scientists on an island off the coast of Costa Rica and hopefully see some prehistoric creatures? Josh shrugged. "Yeah, so long as I don't get eaten."

"Only by mosquitoes," the doctor promised.

Ensconced by magnificent palm trees, the ocean shimmered the deepest tropical turquoise Josh could have imagined.

And if he moved just a bit to the left, he could see the actual beach behind the billboard promoting it. Not bad, a little cloudy, but he couldn't complain.

No, on second thought, he absolutely could. He just shouldn't.

"A bit more touristy than you expected?"

Recognizing the voice, Josh turned to see Dr. Shirakawa walking up to him with a warm smile. He wondered if he would look that fashionable in khaki shorts and a lightweight shirt tied around his midriff.

"Dr. Shirakawa," Josh said, shuffling his luggage around so he could shake her hand. "Pleasure to meet you without the lag time."

"Indeed. And please, you can call me Jane."

"Jane . . . ?" The name came out awkwardly, and Josh decided to avoid further embarrassment. "If it's all right, Dr. Shirakawa is much easier to pronounce."

Odd, for a moment it looked like she was caught in a real life glitch. Either that, or she just stopped to stare at him before shaking her head and leading him through the small town.

"The rainforest on this island," she said, waving at children she seemed friendly with, "is a rich ecosystem filled with opportunities for research. Unfortunately, I'm afraid we scientists have become something of an invasive species."

Josh nodded solemnly. At least, he thought he did. That was the one where you were sad but understanding, he was quite sure.

The majority of the village looked the way he felt a remote jungle village should look, like a recognizable filming location from various 80s adventure movies. That is to say, wooden buildings, unpaved roads with no automobile traffic, stalls overflowing with tropical fruit.

If he listened closely, Josh could almost hear the distant cackle of pre-recorded kookaburras pretending to be local monkeys.

Then there were the billboards, the concrete hotels, the coffee shop named after a *Battlestar Galactica* character.

"We are destroying the ecosystem we have come to study," Dr. Shirakawa said with remorse. "But that's another issue entirely. I'm concerned it's only a matter of time until one of these creatures ends up on the Internet."

Josh raised his eyebrows. "You think these things are smart enough to figure out the Wi-Fi password?"

"What? No? Whatever is going on here, we have the chance to figure it out and maybe stop it now, before every hack pseudoscientist with a YouTube channel tramples all over this ecosystem." She paused. "No offense."

"None taken," Josh assured her, laughing at the idea of him having something as cool as a YouTube channel. "So what are your theories—"

A scream cut through the air.

Josh frowned at the interruption. "What are your theories about—"

Dr. Shirakawa took off, sprinting in the direction of the scream. Josh grumbled and followed.

"What are your theories about the wormholes?" Josh asked when he caught up to the doctor in front of a small hotel.

Dr. Shirakawa must not have heard him, her attention fully on the distraught older woman conversing with her in rapid Spanish. He made out a few words, "Está dentro," but his brain filled in the rest as "[speaking foreign language]."

After saying something presumably comforting to the woman, Dr. Shirakawa nodded her acknowledgement at Josh. "Another pterodactyl. She didn't see where it came from, but it flew past her." Grinning with excitement, she didn't wait to discuss further, pushing through the door with Josh at her heels.

Not much to look at, the lobby. Very storebrand Holiday Inn with the odd flower arrangement for visual interest, but it had air conditioning. Glorious, large-carbon-footprint air conditioning.

The man at the front desk was also not much to look at. Oh, not because he was ugly or ordinary, quite the opposite actually, Josh thought with a twinge of bisexuality. No, just exceptionally skinny and short, literally not much of him to look at. He pointed frantically in the direction the pterodactyl had gone, and only seemed moderately annoyed when Josh left his luggage in a pile in the lobby.

"Theories about the—"

Another shriek. They followed this one to a room, pushing open the door in time to see the end of a scuffle and a maid, armed with a vacuum cleaner hose that honestly looked like it would make a sucky weapon, slamming the bathroom door.

She crossed herself as she tried to catch her breath. Josh didn't understand a word of what she told them, but some things, like "dude there was this little prehistoric guy and I locked it in the bathroom," simply transcend the language barrier.

Dr. Shirakawa put her ear up to the door and listened. She shook her head.

"You can't hear the pterodactyl in the bathroom?" Josh asked.

"No."

"Is that because the P is silent?"

She ignored him. She ignored him even more strongly when she saw that he had tied his shirt into a crop top like hers. "Puedes salir," she said to the maid, who smiled gratefully and left with her vacuum.

Josh opened his mouth.

Dr. Shirakawa held up a finger. "Do not ask me if I have theories about the wormholes."

Josh closed his mouth.

"Find something to protect your hands," she said, going for the door handle. "And a sheet or something to wrap him in."

Josh had concerns about this plan. "I have concerns about this plan," he told her.

"We'll be fine. We got this."

"Do you think there's such a thing as prehistoric rabies?" Josh asked as he bandaged his arm.

"He didn't even bite you," Dr. Shirakawa said, making that frozen video face again. "You fell and cut your arm on the edge of a table."

Josh shrugged. "Just general curiosity."

The doctor just shook her head and went back to documenting the pterodactyl.

And he was truly a pterodactyl. Well, possibly a pteranodon. Some sort of prehistoric flying reptile, in any event.

He had stopped struggling once they had him burrito'd in a pillowcase, but made irritated little noises when Dr. Shirakawa snapped his picture or took measurements. Cute little guy, almost looked like there should have been a puppeteer crouched under the bed operating him.

"Isn't he remarkable?" Dr. Shirakawa marveled.

Josh gave a small shrug. "He's not bad."

The doctor looked at him incredulously. "How can you say that?"

"With my mouth."

"He's about to prove your life's work."

Josh grumbled his agreement. The creature was, indeed, remarkable. A visitor from another time, the ambassador of another world. The announcement would change everything they understood about science.

Well, most things. He assumed a time traveling pterodactyl wouldn't have much of an impact on olfactory ethics, for instance.

"He's just . . . small," Josh told her, lying on the bed with his chin resting on his folded arms so he could stare at the marvelous disappointment. "People will say he's just a weird bird, or a population survived somewhere deep in the jungle. I'm not getting invited on *The Tonight Show* with him, at least not as the first guest. Probably get bumped because Frank Sinatra talked for too long."

Dr. Shirakawa stopped in the middle of a note. "Frank Sinatra is dead."

"That's why they would give him an extra segment if he showed up."

In the silence of Dr. Shirakawa ignoring him, Josh and the pterodactyl studied each other. He was rather remarkable, really. Beautiful amber colored eyes, smooth tan skin with just a few wrinkles here and there, and he looked damn cute with his shirt tied into a crop top.

The pterodactyl wasn't bad, either.

"Just pterodactyls, then?" Josh asked.

"As far as I know, yes."

Interesting. Maybe the other end of the wormhole, wherever and whenever it was, opened in the middle of a nesting site, or in midair.

"No pattern to the appearances?"

The doctor shook her head. "Not that I've been able to find. That's more your area of …" She hesitated, as if about to say "expertise" but thinking better of it. "…interest. Ley lines, sunspots, whatnot."

"You've read my blog."

"I've skimmed it with great enthusiasm," she corrected, tapping him affectionately on the head with her pen as she got up. "This," she said, gesturing to the burritodactyl, "is not a long-term solution. I'm going into town, see if I can find a large birdcage or dog crate, maybe, something for it to eat."

"Carnivore diet," Josh reminded her. "Raw would be best. Chicken maybe? No onions on mine."

Dr. Shirakawa stood there for a moment, her hand on the doorknob as she looked in amazement at the creature. She and Josh shared a giddy grin, and she left the hotel room.

That was the last time Josh ever saw her.

For a little while, Josh tried to find a pattern in the data Dr. Shirakawa had collected. He tried to make it fit his theories, but they all sounded silly, meaningless, in the face of an actual dinosaur-adjacent prehistoric animal sharing a hotel room with him.

Where Pthomas (he had wanted to name him Ptolemy, but had trouble spelling it) came from didn't matter nearly so much as what they would do with him.

And it was odd, Josh thought, idly going through the trash for items he could turn into a little town, anything to keep his hands and brain busy. For so long, he had wanted recognition. He had wanted to go on television and cereal boxes, promoting his discoveries and proving everyone wrong.

Now he had proof. A grumpy little bundle of proof with too many teeth and a hiss like an angry goose. He had proof, and he didn't particularly feel the need to share that with the world.

"I know I was right," he told Pthomas, setting down a cardboard toilet paper tube topped with a paperclip antenna. "I think that might be enough for me. Besides, nobody would believe you eat Wheaties. You can't even hold a spoon."

Maybe they could release him with a tracking collar, follow him back to the wormhole.

Josh looked up at the pterodactyl, who glared down at him and his recyclable city. Pthomas had to go back. Even if they could learn something by studying him, it wouldn't be right to keep him here.

A loud knock on the door startled Pthomas; he cried out in alarm and started struggling to deburrito himself.

"Did you order room service?" Josh asked as he got up and went to open the door. "Because you're paying for it."

It was not, in fact, room service, but rather the unremarkable man from the front desk. He glanced behind Josh but seemed more annoyed at the craft project than the pterodactyl. "Sir," he said with a voice that matched his face, "if you do not intend to book this room, I am going to ask you to leave."

Oh. Right. In all the excitement, Josh and the doctor had neglected to actually pay for the room they had commandeered. He patted his pockets, then remembered his luggage still in the lobby, his wallet containing only American money as he hadn't quite figured out how to exchange it yet.

"I'm just . . ." Josh leaned in the doorway, his intention being to make himself as large as possible and block the view of Pthomas. He realized too late that it seemed like he was flirting, and committed to the bit with a sly smile. "Waiting for my friend."

The man from the front desk raised an eyebrow and looked Josh up and down, his gaze lingering briefly on the exposed midriff. But while Josh did attract the gaze, it seemed he did not attract the gays. "You can wait for her in the lobby. Please vacate this room in the next…" He looked at his watch, checking the check-in time. "Eighteen minutes."

Frowning, Josh watched him leave. He didn't even particularly *want* other men to be attracted to him, it just would have been nice.

Oh well.

"Promise not to bite me if I carry you like a baby until the doctor gets back?" Josh asked, turning around just in time to see Pthomas wriggling free from his burrito and taking flight.

The following few minutes—resulting in several picture frames knocked askew, a broken lamp, and what Josh anticipated would be a nice bruise on his ankle—is best imagined with the *Benny Hill* theme song playing over it.

The chaos culminated with the ancient beast landing in the middle of Josh's recyclable city, stomping on cardboard buildings with a mighty shriek. He flapped his wings and sent an empty can of shaving cream rolling across the room.

"Nice birdy," Josh said in what he hoped was a calming voice. It wasn't accurate, but it sounded better than "Nice prehistoric flying reptile-y."

Pthomas leaped gracefully onto the edge of a dresser, putting his long, toothy snout level with Josh's face, and shrieked again. A full-body scream, wings out and neck extended; with a little movie magic and a green screen, Josh could easily see him towering over a city full of terrified extras.

But he could take a tiny pterodactyl. Yeah, he convinced himself, grabbing a pillowcase in preparation of tackling the creature that probably didn't have prehistoric rabies.

Josh tightened the knot on his shirt, took a couple deep breaths.

But, as they say, when god closes an 18 minute window, he opens a door. Pthomas flew out into the hallway the instant the door opened, Josh running after him.

Josh chased the pterodactyl through the town, his attention so focused that he missed all the details and visual gags in the background, and into the rainforest.

He had seen pictures and videos of environments like this, but it didn't compare to reality.

The trees stretched like the arms of giants, delicate fingertips holding up a thick canopy of green that only let the most cinematic dappled light through. Life surrounded him, plants and animals and too many little bugs, the forest filled with movement and noise.

It smelled natural. Like what the world must have smelled like before humanity ruined it. Perhaps even olfactory ethics could learn a thing or two from the bestseller he would never write.

He didn't see the wormhole itself, but when Pthomas perched on a branch and called out, dozens of other pterodactyls suddenly emerged from somewhere behind Josh. They twirled and danced through the trees, Pthomas falling in with them, and disappeared back to wherever they had come from.

Josh took a moment to stand silently in nature, resisting the urge to swat the mosquitoes trying to steal his DNA. This was not his home, he had no right to impose himself on it.

Josh felt very small and unimportant.

And that is when the dinosaur stepped out from behind a tree. A real, proper dinosaur, a raptor.

The young woman riding the raptor smiled brightly. "Hi. I'm Estella. I need your help to save my people."

Joan of Archaeopteryx

Hallucinations are nothing new to me, but this is my first dinosaur.

Every cell in my body, every scrap of primitive instinct, is screaming for me to grab a pointy stick and take cover in the nearest cave, because I guess my instincts come from an anachronistic Raquel Welch movie where people and dinosaurs coexist.

But I don't let my fear show because, as real as it looks, the logical part of me remembers that dinosaurs are extinct, and that a reaction like that will only confirm that I belong in this hospital. I just have to get through this 72-hour hold, and then I can go home.

So I freak out on the inside, trying to calm my shaking hand that makes my lime Jell-O tremble on the spoon. The knowledge that it isn't real is at war with the competing notion that *it's right there! Right outside the window, being all velociraptor-y in the garden! Lock the doors and windows, hide your Muldoons!*

It has feathers. That's odd. I mean, I guess I know they had feathers, but when I hear "raptor," the image that comes to mind is the scaly, reptilian movie monsters, not this iridescent black bird-looking thing.

And I don't typically imagine them wearing saddles.

I drop my spoon, my heart racing. I briefly forget that I require oxygen to survive, and only remember to breathe when I get lightheaded.

The more details, the harder it is for me to differentiate reality from imagination. Usually, the illusions fizzle away the more I scrutinize them, but this one is getting more detailed and—

Okay, now there's a pretty Latina hallucination chastising the raptor hallucination like it's a bad doggy who ran off after the paper boy, and I am *definitely* not doing well on these new meds.

I squeeze my eyes shut and grip the edge of the table, focusing on the feel of the chipped Formica under my hands. Cool, smooth, real. I inhale the artificial fruity smell of snack time, taste the lime that reminds me of floor cleaner lingering on my tongue.

Then I move on to the senses more likely to be fooled.

I tap my slippers on the floor. It sounds, anticlimactically enough, like I'm tapping my slippers on the floor. No extra noises, no voices other than my fellow residents talking about the latest episode of whatever show they're all obsessed with. . . .

I open my eyes and stare at my lap. Just hospital-issued shapeless pants. Pink, naturally, because we're sorted by gender, which I think is determined by whether they think we got Barbies or Hot Wheels in our Happy Meals as kids.

They put me with the other Barbies. Yeah, I had a few, but I was also a Hot Wheels kid. I guess they don't know what color scrubs that is. Boys are blue, girls are pink, and androgynous-presenting genderqueer assigned female at birth is . . . ?

(It's glitter; our color is glitter.)

Just when I think I'm grounded, that there won't be a dinosaur in full riding tack if I look outside, someone screams.

My head jerks up. The raptor is still there.

And now other people can see it.

Chaos reigns in the lunchroom, residents and orderlies crying out in alarm and pointing out the window.

No, this isn't right. No one else is supposed to see my hallucinations.

One of the orderlies—Bev, who is everything you expect a person named Bev to be and more—apparently decides she isn't going to let something like a velociraptor deny her a much-needed cigarette break, and opens the door to the garden. Hang on, I have to write that again, but in italics so it conveys the right amount of panic.

Bev opens the flipping door that is the only thing separating us, who are delicious and made of meat, from the giant prehistoric murderbird with FEET MADE OF KNIVES!

Now, I'm not the kind of person who runs toward danger, which is why I'm just as surprised as the rest of the lunchroom to find myself running toward the danger. I guess I feel some sort of responsibility. It is *my* hallucination, after all; I wouldn't want it to eat anyone.

(Yeah, I realize my logic leaves a lot to be desired, but hi, I'm Joan, and I'm being held in a psych ward because a voice in my head told me to hurt myself. Thinking clearly isn't exactly one of my strengths at the moment.)

The instant I'm outside, the raptor and its human turn toward me. The girl's face lights up like she's seeing a miracle.

"You!" she calls out, beckoning to me.

Beside me, Bev pauses with the cigarette lighter halfway to her mouth, and I don't even bother to point out that she isn't the designated fifty feet away from the entrance like the signs say she should be. She swears, one of the good ones they bleep out when they show Samuel L. Jackson movies on basic cable, and I realize this is apparently the first time she's even noticed the dinosaur.

"Get inside," I hiss, and she doesn't need to be told twice.

I hear the door lock behind her. She just locked me outside with a dinosaur.

I scramble for a weapon, but the staff doesn't exactly leave sharp objects lying around where patients can reach them. Just when I decide to run for my life, the rider calls out to me.

"He won't hurt you! He's tame!"

Right. People say the same thing about ferrets, but there's a world of difference between "tame" and "I trapped this fancy weasel in my house so it's mine now."

"Please." Her voice cracks, and she clings to the raptor's reins with desperation. "We need your help."

Ignoring the dinosaur factor for the moment, who could possibly need *my* help? I'm no one. I'm nothing.

But the desire to help burns bright in my heart, like a calling. It's probably just one of my delusions of grandeur, but I want to be wanted. I need to be needed. I . . . think I'm ripping off a Cheap Trick song, but that's irrelevant.

I know, somewhere deep inside, that this is as close to a purpose as I'm ever going to get.

So I follow the pretty girl and her dinosaur around the corner and through a portal.

Estella is under the impression that I am in a position to absorb information, and calmly chatters on like any of this is remotely okay.

"—but then of course the savior got eaten by an allosaur, leaving me in *quite* a sticky situation, as you can understand. But I think—"

"You're riding a velociraptor," I interrupt. I want to believe this is all some enormous hallucination, but I don't think it is. I've never had tactile hallucinations before, and the rain pouring down on my head feels too real, too cold as it sticks my hospital-issue clothing to my skin.

And like I said, I don't usually hallucinate dinosaurs, but everywhere I look, the world is a giant natural history museum mural. A herd of brontosaurs graze in the valley below, and I swear I'm hearing the John Williams Orchestra. (Okay, *that* one is probably a hallucination.)

"Utahraptor," Estella corrects, wiping dark, rain-plastered hair off her forehead. "But yes. We've been over this already."

The raptor—Malcolm, she called him—nudges my arm with his wet, feathery cheek like we're BFFs.

"I think I need you to go over it again," I say numbly, sitting on a rock and covering my face with my hands.

Estella groans softly at the delay in getting wherever it is we're going, but she stops beside me and complies. "Not all dinosaurs went extinct. Some escaped into another world—this world, Avalonia. Sometimes portals open between them. In the 1800s, people discovered the portals when utahraptors started nomming on their cattle. My great great—maybe there's a third great, I can't remember—aunt was the first to ride one, and a small town called Hell Creek rode them for a couple years."

"Which isn't in the history books because...?" I ask, trying to ground myself in the raindrops and the smell of petrichor and the . . . distant trumpets of hadrosaurs. Okay, so that didn't work.

"Because . . . *reasons*," Estella says with reverence. "The first modern people to come through a portal were my several-greats-grandfather and his sister Rosita and about half their town, and fast forward a bunch of years, and we're at war with the descendants of the people who pretended they came through during the Renaissance—"

"Insert 'dinosaur renaissance' joke here," I murmur.

"—and there's a prophecy that someone will come through a portal and lead us to victory. Which totally came true last week! His name was Josh and he was *so* cool."

I look up at her. I remember this part from the first time she told me the story. "And then you got him eaten."

She slumps in her saddle. "And then I got him eaten." She perks back up, because she is apparently the living embodiment of a Weeble whose theme song is "Tubthumping." "But now you're here! Admittedly, I was hoping for a guy, but. . . ." She gestures vaguely at all of me.

She means I have a boyish frame. Which would be a compliment if we weren't in a *Land Before Time* movie. (Oh god, I hope it's the first movie and not one of the sequels with all the singing.)

"So, what do you want from me?" I ask, but a crashing sound in the treeline swivels our attention thataway.

Before I can respond, Estella and her raptor are off like a shot, and she's got a sword, and *I* want a sword; why don't I have a sword?

The treeline erupts in movement; half a dozen raptors and riders charge through the rain, screaming and screeching and holding maroon and gold banners aloft like a medieval army. One falls as Estella slashes at them, her raptor skirting nimbly out of the reach of the blades on their powerful back legs.

The five remaining riders turn their raptors in sync, and Estella and Malcolm take slow steps backward. She's still grinning, but it falters.

There's no way she can handle them all by herself.

I glance at the fallen rider, who's been abandoned by his injured raptor as it fled into the forest. He's got a crossbow.

Now, I'm a lot of things. Nerd, queer, mentally ill. One thing I'm not is an archer, but I guess that's about to change.

I scurry across the slick grass and make the mistake of locking eyes with the fallen man as I take his bow.

He is . . . not as dead as I hoped he would be, because this isn't a video game and bad guys don't die as soon as you wound them, even if their insides are kinda mostly outsides now. Should I say something? I think I should say something.

"Um. Any tips on how to use your bow?"

His only answer is a sad gurgle, so I'm on my own. But I watch *The Walking Dead*; I know how to use a crossbow.

Spoiler: I do not know how to use a crossbow. Like at all.

On the bright side, as the arrow-bolt-thingy flies ineffectually straight up and lands about twenty feet to the right of the nearest enemy, it draws their attention firmly in my direction and distracts them from Estella. So . . . yay me?

I consider holding perfectly still, but don't think that will help anything. "Next one won't miss!" I shout instead, pretending to be a badass in soaking pink hospital clothes.

Estella gets one of them while they're busy being stunned by my brilliance (I guess? I really don't understand why they're so freaked out), and Malcolm swipes his claws across another raptor's flank, almost starting a skirmish until the rider pulls his dinosaur away.

One of them holds their hands up as they dismount. I raise the bow to my eye, then realize I don't even have an arrow in it, but they can't see that in the staticky curtain of rain. They go to their fallen comrade, sling his body over the back of an uninjured mount, and they all disappear into the trees as fast as they had appeared.

Estella whoops in joy.

"What was that?" I yell.

"You look exactly like Josh! They must've been the same ones who were there when he got eaten! They think you're him, and immortal, like the prophecy says!"

The adrenaline rush dissipates, and I sink to the ground because I can't rely on my legs for support.

"*That's* what I want from you. Pretend to be Josh—I haven't exactly broken the news to anyone back home that he's been eaten—and give them hope. That's all we need—just a little morale boost."

Dress like a man? Cut my hair, bind my chest, have adventures, and never be called "ma'am"?

"Okay, but I want a sword."

I would have thought being a savior in a land of dinosaurs would be more exciting. Mostly it's a lot of waving from the balcony of the administrative building in New Hell Creek, a quaint, pseudo-Old-West deal with the odd modern amenity like indoor plumbing, gay pride flags hanging from the tailor shop, and, bizarrely, a helicopter with an archaeopteryx painted over the original logo of some company apparently starting with the letter E.

The people here are a lot like the town, mixed and matched from various time periods and locations. Different skin tones, religions, all sorts of genders and orientations, but they accept one another. And they're all terrified of what happens if they lose this war.

But then they see me, and there's hope. They truly believe I'm going to save them.

Even with my spiffy new haircut and boy clothes, I don't look enough like Josh to fool anyone at close range. So here I sit in a fantastic parallel universe, a savior, doodling the archaeopteryx on the tricolor flag and trying to memorize the spelling of "archaeopteryx" so I don't look like a *total* doof.

But I did get a sword, so yay me. (I say sarcastically, rewrapping the gauze on my hand. Swords are sharp.)

I go to the library a lot, in disguise, mostly to convince myself that this is all real.

I like dinosaurs. I'm ambivalent toward, but knowledgeable about, history. But there's no way I know enough about either to fill all these lovingly handbound tomes with obscure dinos and their impact on world events.

Opening a page at random, I find that Amelia Earhart and her navigator disappeared when they flew through a portal that happened to open at high altitude. Another page, and it's all about the Jersey Devil being some sort of pterosaur I can't even pronounce. Something about D.B. Cooper. . . . And here's a whole bunch of math about why the portals open when they do. . . .

I'm smart, but I'm not "make up random shit that looks like quantum mechanics" smart, and my hallucinations have never been this immersive before, so I'm inclined to believe it's really happening.

Which means these people are real, they can really die, and they really expect me to have some part in preventing that.

Okay, I can do this.

"I can't do this," I tell Estella. My hands shake so bad, I have to press them against each other to keep them still.

She nods to indicate she heard me but makes no comment as she continues to clean the blood off the raptor bridle in her lap. Human or prey animal? I don't dare ask.

The stables are nearly silent, most of the raptors having been turned out to hunt for the day. Only a few scratches of claw on sawdust betray that anyone is behind those great steel doors.

Most of this town was built by Estella's ancestors, who came through from the 1800s, but the doors are a more modern touch. A necessity, given the strength of the dinosaurs. At least they don't have the kind of handle that we all know raptors can open.

Except they *don't* all know that. I haven't seen a single electrical outlet in town, let alone a TV/VCR combo with a VHS of *Jurassic Park*, despite this world definitely having the capability to build an electrical grid.

Estella told me that Camelops knights have been known to target anything resembling modern tech and destroy it.

Makes sense, from what I've read about them. It used to be worse, but Camelops still acts like they fancy themselves the Rulers of All and resist progress like typical Dark Age jerks who escaped to this world when the Middle Ages were getting a little *too* progressive.

They didn't. They were regular people from my century who lied until it became the truth, and somehow that makes it so much worse. The people who live there truly believe that their hatred evolved naturally instead of being twisted into existence, the gaps in logic filled in with problematic frog DNA.

They don't want women to own property, they'd persecute us queers as witches if they had their way. . . . They even call the dinosaurs "dragons" because they refuse to believe that god would let a creature He created go extinct.

"I agree they need to be defeated," I continue to Estella. "But your people expect me to plan *battles*. I don't know if you realize, but I was in a mental institution on a three-day hold because the voices in my head told me to—"

She sets the tack down on a table, the metal pieces clattering. "I don't know if *you* realize," she says, standing and stepping forward until we're nearly nose to nose, "but we're losing this war." Her bubbly perkiness is gone, replaced by a rage I didn't know she was capable of. "My ancestors came here to find freedom to live as they wanted. And now it's going to be taken away."

A raptor warbles down the hall, upset by the tension in her voice.

Me too, buddy.

"Look. I didn't make up this prophecy, and I don't believe in it, but a lot of people do and I inherited the responsibility of protecting that. They need to believe that some guy from your world is going to come and save them. They need hope, Joan, and I got their last hope killed. If we lose this war, it will be my fault that we lose the right to believe what we want and love who we love and be whatever gender makes our hearts sing."

She crosses her fingers and kisses them, then raises her hands to indicate the barn, and the town beyond its walls.

"All of this could be gone tomorrow if they invade, because we don't have the numbers to fight them off. So I don't care if you hear voices. I don't care if you don't think you can do this. You're going to be our savior because we need you." Her voice grows tight at the end as she fights back the tears shimmering in her eyes like an inconsolable schoolgirl in an anime.

I don't know what to say so I just hug her. I'm not really a hugger, but it's a good way to hide my tears.

I'm not a hero. I'm just some person wearing men's clothes and a breast binder, pretending to know what I'm doing.

Seriously. When they ask for my input on battles, I'm literally just quoting strategy guides from *Final Fantasy* games. "Long-range weapons in the back," I say, stroking the stubble I've drawn on with an eyebrow pencil. "Melee in the front along with those with the best shields."

I dread the day I accidentally call their raptors "Chocobos."

"I don't know how," I tell Estella, "but I'll find a way."

Even as I make the promise, I'm afraid I'm going to let everyone down.

Pro-tip: Riding horses a couple times in middle school doesn't mean you can just sit on a utahraptor, click your tongue, and off you go on a *Saddle Club* adventure.

I mean, a trail ride at camp fifteen years ago doesn't even make you qualified to do that on a *horse*, and a utahraptor is about the farthest you can get from a horse without being a suspension bridge.

For one thing, they're predators. I'm reminded of this fact when my first lesson goes horribly wrong, and my mount, a sparrow-brown male named Dennis, goes charging into the woods after an archaeopteryx. With me on his back.

I hold on for dear life, ducking as he sprints under branches and over rocks while Estella's laughs fade in the distance.

I don't think I fully appreciated the pure muscle these creatures are made of until just now, but Dennis explodes with power with each step like an annoying person who always talks about the gym can only dream of. Not that this changes a damn thing, but at least it's a nice distraction from the *runaway half-ton knife-turkey I'm riding!*

That's the other thing about riding raptors. Between their teeth and their sickle claws, they're like ninety percent sharp edges. Even if the raptor does everything you ask and doesn't try to hurt you . . . it's probably still going to hurt you.

For that reason, I'm in what amounts to a full suit of armor, kevlar and leather up and down my limbs and a helmet obscuring my face. It will help if I fall, but—call me crazy (you won't be the first)—the idea of falling off a speeding raptor just doesn't strike me as a great idea.

So I duck and hold on for dear life as we thrash through the woods, startling birds and squirrels and little unidentified dinosaurs.

When we finally slow to a stop and I pick my head up, the archeopteryx is gone and the sun-dappled forest has been replaced by a bright field full of mounted pseudo-Ren-Faire soldiers.

Dennis chirps a short, sharp syllable, the raptor equivalent of a curse word. I translate under my breath.

But no one shoots me, no one flees in horror at my Josh-has-risen-ness. I look at their armor—most are covered in fancy tunics, but a few wear bare kevlar like mine, despite their supposed hatred of modern tech—and I realize that they think I'm one of them.

"Preston!" barks a man in full maroon and gold regalia, his iridescent black raptor positively dripping in velvet and sashes. He raises the visor of his helmet—an old school Sir Lancelot tin can dealie—and squints as if he's not quite sure who I am. With an army the size of his, there's no way he knows everyone by heart.

I snap to attention, holding the reins tightly and praying that Dennis will behave. "Sir!" I say in my deepest manly man voice. If Camelops punishes women for daring to want control over their uteri, I think it's safe to say they don't let uterus-havers in the military.

"Any sign of the cowboys?"

I hear rustling behind me. Estella, no doubt, coming after me. I raise my voice and hope Preston doesn't have a strong New Zealand accent or something. "No, sir! No sign of the enemy!"

I don't dare look behind me to see if she's still there. Hopefully she's savvy enough to figure out what I'm doing.

Which is what, exactly? Becoming a spy?

Estella didn't exaggerate anything about the kingdom of Camelops. This place is like if Medieval Times was designed for maximum toxic masculinity.

(Yeah, I feel like a man sometimes, but my masculinity doesn't come with a label urging you to contact your local poison control center if ingested.)

These people ride dinosaurs. They live in castles. They wear doofy knight outfits and use trumpeting parasaurolophuses with streamers dangling from their crests to herald the arrival of their king and queen.

It should be whimsical. It should be fun.

And yet I honestly believe that they will burn me at the stake if they learn what parts my body has.

I managed to keep my helmet on until I got back to the army barracks, where I dyed my hair with some ink so no one would mistake me for Josh, but I can't wear my binder forever and I have a feminine face. It's only a matter of time until someone figures it out, and then put on a punny apron and put some potato salad in a cheap bowl you don't mind never getting back, because it's barbecue time.

I'm the last one to go to bed, and I can't bring myself to close my eyes, so I just stare at the dark ceiling until the knots in the wood come alive.

I never thought my hallucinations could be comforting, but the sight of giant spiders crawling above my bed almost makes me weep with joy, because they're just so damn harmless. They're a memento of a world where I might not have been adored or supported, but I was never really in danger from anyone but myself.

No one back home ever made me afraid to be myself. Yeah, I lived in a relatively safe area, and of course hate crime is a thing, but I never once lay awake at night worrying that I would be arrested or executed if someone found out I was hiding my boobs.

Exhaustion makes it easier to hear the voices.

Once upon a time, they told me I was worthless, and I believed them. Tonight, it's mostly chatter. White noise that helps me forget about the dinosaurs and the war.

I interpret it as a pep talk.

All those hours in the library are about to pay off.

I've kept my head down, my mouth shut, and my boobs hidden for almost a week. Biding my time, using war games to bond with Dennis while I figured out a strategy.

I'll admit, I was skeptical about the whole "I'm going to sit on this here murder-emu and hope it doesn't eat me" thing, but raptors are smart (clever, you could say) and social. As long as you keep it fed and don't piss it off by poking it with a pointy stick, a well-raised raptor is like a Doberman: yes, it can kill you, but it knows its loyalty and love will go further than violence.

Once Dennis realized I was going to be good to him, he started behaving, and now he responds to my commands with a practiced ease. With just a subtle shift of my body weight, I direct him to slow as we come up alongside our fellow knights in the valley.

Adrenaline prickles at my skin, my rapid breaths echoing metallically in my helmet.

It was my intel that brought us here, my reports of "overheard conversations" in the woods. If it goes wrong, if I misremembered even part of the attack I helped plan, or the dates and locations in the books. . . .

But the voices in my head tell me it'll be okay, and they're all I've got at the moment, so I'm going to have to believe them.

A hundred raptors shift from foot to taloned foot, chittering with excitement. This is it, most of their cavalry is right here. If we can take them out, the rest will fall.

The war ends today.

I realize they're all looking at me. I might be a nobody knight— so forgettable that they've forgotten my name several times, switching from Preston to Warner and now Lakewood—but I was the one who spoke up, who called out their generals and came up with a better plan.

And it didn't hurt that I had all sorts of dirt on the king, thanks to a book from the library. Spoiler: he's not a wizard like he says he is, and is, in fact, D.B. Cooper.

So a little military strategy, a little blackmail, and bippidy boppidy brontosaurus, I'm leading a freaking army.

Or, technically, I'm sitting motionlessly at the front of a freaking army. I should change that.

Do I... do I say something? Charge ahead and hope they follow? What are the chances my army of parallel universe Dark Agers is familiar with the "They can't take away our FREEEE-DOM!" speech from *Braveheart*?

"Okay, people," I call out for want of a better war cry. "Hold onto your butts!"

We charge, a hundred pairs of talons tearing at the grass and dirt as we come over the crest of the hill en masse. The thrill of battle thrums through me, and for a second I almost forget that they're the enemy, that they would kill me as soon as look at me if they knew who I am and what I'm really fighting for.

It just feels right, somewhere deep inside me. I can't shoot a bow or swing a sword for shit and the thought of actually injuring someone makes me queasy, but I love the feeling of camaraderie, false as it may be.

It sure beats lime Jell-O and psych ward scrubs.

Aside from a few grazing hadrosaurs, the adjacent valley is devoid of life, in direct contrast to the army I said would be there.

Some of my soldiers fall back, shouting that we're being ambushed, but most follow me and Dennis, faster, faster, must go faster down the hill, so fast they won't be able to stop in time.

They are absolutely being ambushed, but not by another army. By *knowledge*.

That confusing physics book from the library? It had an appendix filled with pages and pages of predicted times and locations of portal openings. And one is going to open right...

I lean hard to the side, turning my raptor at a sharp angle.

...NOW.

Too sharp an angle. I lose my balance, toppling sideways in the saddle. I grab at the reins but too late; I hit the ground, little cartoon archaeopteryxes twirling around my dazed head.

I'm vaguely aware of a whooshing, and the panicked shouts that dwindle into nothingness as the army tries and fails to stop their raptors from charging straight into the opening portal. To paraphrase Isaac Newton, momentum's a bitch.

Have fun in the actual Cretaceous, ya Ren Faire rejects.

The portal closes as quickly as it opened. Not everyone went through, but Estella's people actually are nearby. They will have heard all the commotion.

Gunshots confirm it; they're coming to pick off the stragglers. Between the Camelops army's low numbers and this morale boost, it'll be over soon.

We won.

Dennis, realizing that I'm still lying in the grass, comes over to nuzzle me, his snuffling breath hot and smelling of dead things. I laugh, giddy at the world. There's a utahraptor inches from my face, a utahraptor who I've *ridden like a pony*, and I just led an army and won a war in a parallel universe.

I grasp his halter and let him help pull me to my feet. In a distant way, I notice something parting the shoulder-height grass surrounding us.

I don't realize the implications of this until the bowman reveals himself and an arrow embeds itself in my shoulder.

A strange thrumming sound wakes me.

The ceiling above me is clinically white, and for one terrifying moment, I think I'm back at the hospital and this was all some hallucination.

I can't go back to that world.

That world tried to kill me, tried to drug away my problems, but the voices aren't my problem. I can deal with them if I have a purpose and somewhere that I fit in. They're still here, in Estella's world, but they're harmless.

Then I worry I've been captured. I'm not wearing my armor. Did they see—

"She's awake!"

Estella.

My relieved laughter turns to sobs that jostle my injured shoulder. I cherish that pain, because it means it was all real.

"Did we win?"

She grins. "We did."

I fall back. "Don't make me go home."

"Joan, my town is for people like you. People who don't fit in back where they come from." Estella gently touches my face. "You're already home."

I close my eyes again as the helicopter lifts off and heads back to New Hell Creek, and quietly hum the *Jurassic Park* theme.

Polter-Gastonia

"**G**astonia?"

Mr. Scott read the word aloud as if it had personally insulted his mother, or perhaps as if he was insulting his mother himself. Rosalinda couldn't quite tell.

"Yes, sir. It's like an ankylosaurus but without the—" She made a fist and swung it like a tail club, and then quickly scrambled to catch the very heavy and therefore expensive vase she almost swept off his desk. Her hands stayed behind her back for the rest of the conversation. "About the size of a really long Shetland pony shaped like a turtle."

Mr. Scott looked at Rosalinda over the tablet, which she had brought to him directly like an extra in *Star Trek* instead of simply emailing him the report. "They're naming these lizards after Disney princes now?"

His ability to be wrong about so many things with so few words was truly baffling.

"It wasn't. . . . They aren't. . . . Gaston isn't—"

One might say Mr. Scott interrupted her, but that would imply he had been at all aware that Rosalinda was speaking. "Is it worth the expense to excavate?"

Before she answered, Rosalinda had to translate his question into what he was actually asking: was it impressive enough to be a status symbol or something he could sell for substantial money?

"No, sir," she said reluctantly.

Mr. Scott handed the tablet back with a dismissive wave of his hand. "Then we're moving forward with construction."

Rosalinda's heart shattered like the vase almost had.

The fossil beds may not have contained anything of monetary value, but to the scientific community they could be priceless. How could he care so little about the pursuit of knowledge, about the insight they could gain into the prehistoric world where mammals scurried around beneath the feet of giants and the evolution of humans was an impossible dream? And the fossil bed was dangerously close to the ghost town of Hell Creek—

"Are you still here?" Mr. Scott asked suddenly, looking up from his phone.

"Yes, sir," Rosalinda apologized.

"Fix that."

"Yes, sir."

She briefly entertained the idea of sweeping the vase off his desk on her way out, but that wouldn't have been fair to the artisans who made it, even if they were long dead.

In the grand scheme of things, Rosalinda thought as she stared at her ceiling and waited for her ADHD to let her brain settle enough for sleep, Mr. Scott wasn't an evil man.

He didn't go out of his way to spread misery, it just affected everyone with the misfortune to interact with him. He would never purposely inflict suffering on any person or creature, he even saved spiders and released them outside, but if suffering happened and it benefited him to let it continue, he would pretend not to see it. A month earlier, it had taken every employee going on strike and halting business entirely for a week for him to even meet with the electrical worker union about safety concerns, but he took them seriously once the bad PR forced him to, and only spared some expense implementing changes.

So not evil, at least not compared to some, but merely bad, with enough money and influence to affect the world.

"So it'd be wrong to kill him," Rosalinda said to herself. "Probably." And then, just in case the government or her phone was listening in, she added, "Definitely."

Not that she would. Even if he really truly deserved it, she didn't have or want the right to make that determination. It was just nice to think about sometimes, like being a wizard or kissing Tom Baker or running away into that secret rip in time and space her family had been protecting since half the population of Hell Creek went through there to start a new life.

She picked at her fingernails, purple polish flaking onto her partner's shirt she wore as pajamas. The fossil bed was too close to the ghost town and its intermittent portal. He would just keep expanding, destroying, and conquering, and eventually Electrum Industries bulldozers would come to Hell Creek.

"Wish this was a horror movie," Rosalinda said to herself and possibly the government, though she suspected they had far more interesting people they could spy on. "Then the ghosts would scare the corrupt developer out of building on their burial ground."

She stopped. Pondered. She could have merely thought or considered, but this situation definitely called for pondering.

Yes.

Yes, she needed to make this a horror movie.

Procuring the dinosaur wasn't what Rosalinda would consider easy by any stretch of the imagination, but seeing as gastonia had gone extinct before the first grass had evolved on Earth, she supposed it wasn't as difficult as it could've been.

The portal to Avalonia had opened more or less on schedule, as predicted by statistics and math based on the pioneering work of Lindy Roman. From there it was merely a matter of finding someone who kept gastonia, bartering about the price, and wrangling the subadult into the horse trailer.

Hell Creek, both the rapidly growing civilization and the fading ghost in the desert, spoke to her heart in ways Rosalinda hadn't anticipated. They felt like coming home, even though keeping watch over the portal was really more her cousin's thing and so she had never visited before today.

"I need to come back here more often," she told the dinosaur, whom she had been able to rent at a surprisingly cheap price, paid in gadgets and foodstuffs unavailable in Avalonia as the society had no use for Earth currency.

It seemed the triangular spikes protruding from the dinosaur's front shoulders, combined with a supposed easygoing attitude, made this species popular with people trying to clear a path through thick brush on their property. Seemed, and supposed, Rosalinda thought, wondering if Avalonia had anything resembling Yelp where she could leave a less than glowing review.

(Conveniently located a short carriage ride from New Hell Creek, Cotillon Terrace offers a small but varied selection of prehistoric creatures available for hire. Whether you need a pair of aurochs to pull a farm plow, or just a spiky boy to scare your boss into being just a bit less of an unethical asshole, you'll probably find it on this sprawling farm. The owner seems to care about the animals, and is more than willing to haggle, but I should've paid him in dictionaries because he does not know what "calm" or "obedient" mean, please see attached pictures of all the bruises on my legs from trying to get this thing in my trailer. Also he kept trying to rent me a plesiosaurus. Sir, I live in Utah? Why would I need one of those? 2 1/2 stars.)

But Rosalinda couldn't complain. Not really, not in any serious way.

Uncooperative and made of blunt force objects as she may have been, there was a dinosaur standing before Rosalinda. A living, breathing, breathtakingly magnificent dinosaur, staring into her eyes as she stared back.

She wasn't meant to see this creature; no human was.

It gave her goosebumps; she didn't feel worthy. What was that thing her partner's family did at church, the sign of the cross? Rosalinda started to attempt it, hesitated upon realizing muscle memory was pressuring her to do the Macarena instead, and ultimately decided to hold her hands reverently behind her back.

"Let's go terrify a millionaire."

Mr. Scott woke the next morning blissfully unaware that he was in a horror movie.

Oh, he noticed some odd occurrences as he dressed in a suit that cost more than Rosalinda's tax bracket and had breakfast at an empty table that could seat a dozen. Of course he noticed; who wouldn't notice a trail of desert soil across the floor, or mysterious scratches in the wall at precisely the height of a gastonia shoulder spike?

He just utterly failed to recognize them as foreshadowing.

At first, anyway.

Once he left his penthouse and headed toward the site in his limo, the reminders began popping up on his phone. Reminders he didn't set, each consisting only of a dimly lit fossilized dinosaur skull that seemed to stare directly at him with empty, gaping eyes.

The third reminder came with a message:

SOON

At which point he promptly called Rosalinda.

"I'm sorry Mr. Scott," she said, feigning confusion while giving Zara the unimpressed gastonia a conspiratorial grin. "What exactly is happening with your phone?"

"Skulls," he repeated, and she couldn't tell if she imagined a bit of fear under his annoyance. "Dinosaur skulls. Not even the good ones, just some goofy iguana with a big forehead."

Rosalinda covered the microphone and mouthed, "I told you he's a jerk." Gingerly, she held out another apple slice and let Zara take it from her fingers. She flicked her flashlight on and then off. "Sounds fun, what app is this?"

"I'm being threatened!" he shouted. "Someone hacked my phone, they may have tampered with my apartment. Rosalinda, pull up a list of employees with your level of access or higher, see if there are any who oppose the development at the fossil site."

It wasn't that Mr. Scott trusted Rosalinda so much as that he gave her so little thought, the notion of whether he could or should trust her had simply never occurred to him.

This was, as it turned out, a recurring problem with Mr. Scott. He paid no attention to those he deemed background characters in his life, merely gave them tasks he had no desire to accomplish him-self. (This had resulted, many years ago, in an employee stealing his private helicopter. It was apparently not a learning experience for Mr. Scott.)

Thus he had forgotten adding Rosalinda to his reminders app, forgotten giving her the key to his apartment several weeks ago, and forgotten entirely what his driver looked like.

"I don't know," Rosalinda said, shifting out of the way as Zara plopped down in the shade of the rocky outcropping. "Sounds like a ghost to me."

She texted her partner while Mr. Scott sputtered about the absurdity of this, and Sunday immediately slammed on the brakes in the limousine.

"Did you see that?"

He had not, and in fact, looking frantically out the windows now was the first time he realized they had traded civilization for dusty highways and sandstone scrubland that reached toward the distant mountains. "See what?"

Sunday poured all of their community theater experience into their performance, hands shaking as they turned the wheel, driving the limousine off the road. "I can't, it was—god, the way it looked right at us!"

"What was it?" Mr. Scott demanded.

Rather than answering, Sunday stopped suddenly, looking in the rearview mirror. "Oh god, get out of the car, get out of the car!"

Caught up in the adrenaline and fear, Mr. Scott scrambled out of the limousine and watched in horror as Sunday called out, "I'm sorry, I have a family!" and drove away.

Astute readers may have noticed the recurring theme of Mr. Scott paying no attention to things he thought could or perhaps should be handled by others. As such, it should come as no surprise that he had never been to the dig site he intended to build on, nor did he know exactly what a paleontological dig looked like.

It had not been difficult for Rosalinda and Sunday to make a convincing fake. A couple canvas tents, some plastic femurs from old Halloween skeletons sticking out of the ground, and they had the stage set for Mr. Scott to play their unwitting Mr. Scrooge.

Rosalinda and Zara waited backstage, a peaceful understanding having been reached over their mutual love of snacks and sitting in the shade while expending as little energy as possible. Their part came later. For now, the ghosts of Cretaceous past and present had a date with Mr. Scott.

Dressed as he was in his expensive suit designed with air conditioned boardrooms in mind, walking down the road to find the nearest convenience store was an option Mr. Scott found as distasteful as most people found him. So while he waited for someone, anyone, to check their voicemail and retrieve him (an unlikely occurrence as his employees had all received an email granting them a surprise day off), he sought refuge from the oppressive heat under a canvas canopy.

He would never admit to being spooked by . . . whatever had just happened, though it was a bit unsettling that the dirt underfoot seemed to be the same color as that which had been mysteriously tracked through his apartment. And he would never admit how high he jumped when the tablet with the cracked screen beside him suddenly started playing an audio recording.

"We aren't the first," whispered Sunday in a British accent. "I've been reading about these gentlemen from the 1800s, Cope and Marsh. They started a paleontological war, cared more about beating the other than the science, and destroyed fossils rather than let each other find them. All those skeletons, all the potential research, gone forever because of greed."

"That's all true," Rosalinda told Zara. "The next part isn't, but it should be."

"I read some of their diaries," Sunday continued, and hidden speakers around Mr. Scott played the occasional guttural snarl. "The same thing that's happening to us, the footprints, the bones. . . . god, I think it's outside right now. I can hear it scraping the Jeep."

Mr. Scott looked up, noticed a Jeep with a deep gouge in the paint identical to the ones in his hallway. He started breathing faster. He didn't know how to be a prey animal, but he felt like one for the first time in his life.

The rest of the recording consisted of screaming, crashing, and then static.

It was evening when the ghost of Cretaceous future finally appeared. Rosalinda wanted to wait until nighttime proper, but it was dark enough now and she couldn't be sure how much battery Mr. Scott had used, cowering in the corner of the tent and checking his phone every few minutes.

She sent him the website using an anonymous number, a fake news article dated five years in the future. It detailed the disastrous events that had befallen Electrum Industries, attributing it to vengeful prehistoric ghosts.

At the bottom of the article, they listed extinct species that could once be found at the dig site but were now lost forever to history.

The final species, the American businessman, showed a picture of Mr. Scott.

"Ready?" Rosalinda asked Zara, who made an irritated noise at the prospect of getting up but reluctantly did so.

Rosalinda touched up the animal-safe glow-in-the-dark paint and led the dinosaur out from behind the outcropping. In the distance, Sunday flicked on their flashlight, a signal Rosalinda had spent the last day and a half associating with Zara's favorite snack.

Mr. Scott did not see a joyful dinosaur galloping toward the promise of delicious apples. All he saw was a ghostly apparition of a glowing skeleton with blades on its shoulders, charging straight at him.

Sunday's voice came over the speakers, emotionless and yet somehow regretful at the same time. "They don't want us here. They want to be left alone. It's too late for us. I fear for the people who just bought the land for development, if they don't learn to respect the dead."

Whether or not Mr. Scott heard that warning over the sound of his own screaming is anyone's guess.

The development still happened, just elsewhere and with a significant delay. But the fossil bed was preserved, and the secret of Hell Creek stayed a secret a little longer.

Mr. Scott never really became a good person, but he was more tolerable and made significantly fewer (not zero, but fewer) heartless villain business decisions. Rosalinda decided that was good enough for now. They had fought the battle, let someone else fight the war, she thought, snuggling with Sunday the next evening.

"Did you hear about this?" Sunday asked, reading the news from their phone.

"Hear about what?" Rosalinda mumbled into her shirt that looked quite good on Sunday.

"Some Scottish asshole is building something on Loch Ness and it's totally screwing with the ecosystem."

Rosalinda perked up. "I happen to know where we can rent a plesiosaur. And I have a coupon."

Don't Cry for Me Argentinosaurus

"**I** can explain."

The sauropod closes her eyes briefly and lets out a quiet snort of hot air that blows Veronica's curls out of her face. People say she personifies them too much, makes them sound like *Land Before Time* characters instead of real animals, but she still thinks of that snort as Gertie's version of rolling her eyes in exasperation.

"Yeah, I know." She leans her forearms on the old familiar balcony and looks past Gertie, out at everything she ruined. "But we have a solution. I promise."

She didn't mean to run away to the real world any more than she had meant to run *away* from it all those years ago, but then the portal opened.

Veronica stared at it, the shimmering crack in reality she had spent years looking for. And now here it was, appearing only after she had decided to make herself a future in this strange land trapped in the past.

Gertie started toward the portal but Veronica hooked an arm around her skinny neck.

"No," she said in response to the dinosaur's vocalizations of protest, setting down the basket of leaves she had been bringing to the pharmacist in town. "No, my world isn't a good place for you. They would put you in a zoo on an island 120 miles west of Costa Rica, and there are several movies about why that's a bad idea."

The portal glimmered in the sunlight, beckoning, promising all the things that should have come with adulthood. Friends, a career, nice clothes and a car and dates and . . . and not this. Not loneliness, foraging, bartering for clothes, and the occasional bout of running for her life from a pack of raptors.

Gertie bellowed softly, resting her chin on the top of Veronica's head.

"I'm not leaving you," Veronica promised, and to her credit, she thought she was telling the truth, she thought it was her decision to make. "I'm just going to peek through, see what the world looks like. I'll be right back."

If you aren't looking at just the right angle, and if you don't expect to see an interdimensional portal on the shoulder of the highway, there's a very good chance it will go unnoticed for the duration of its brief existence. A young woman suddenly stepping out of it, however . . . that is considerably more difficult to ignore, as San Diego's morning rush-hour discovered.

And just like that, any hope of sneaking back through fizzled away like fog in the sunlight. Or like the portal itself, dissolving before her panicked eyes.

They dressed her up like a pinup girl from *The Flintstones*. Leopard print bikini top and matching sarong with jagged edges, jewelry made from plastic teeth and claws, just the right amount of mud tastefully applied to her bare feet.

"You all know I had real clothes, right?" Veronica asked, resisting the urge to swat away the stylist affixing a small bone to one of the braids in her otherwise meticulously messy hair. The beginnings of a migraine throbbed at her temple; the medications here were a joke compared to the tonics back home. "When I came back, I was wearing jeans and a Madonna t-shirt. I had shoes, and I—"

She pointed at one of the production assistants, who was proudly carrying a spear. "No. Absolutely not."

"Veronica," the nice middle-aged man who had insisted on being her publicist said quietly.

"Tony," she said, frowning as one of the makeup artists insisted on fixing her eyebrows yet again.

"The article will tell your story, the pictures are just...." He made a vague gesture. "It's a metaphor. Symbolism. It's like Jerry Seinfeld holding a rubber chicken."

"Jerry Seinfeld doesn't have to dress like a neanderthal go-go dancer," Veronica pointed out. At least, she was pretty sure he didn't. A lot could've changed in the last ten years.

She had missed so much. All the movies and world events, the shared joys and despairs everyone around her had experienced together while she was out running around with dinosaurs.

She started breathing harder, faster, squinting at the bright lights and fussing with the necklace that was feeling tighter with every passing second. This time, she did swat away the hand reaching for her face.

"No!"

"Hey." Tony nodded toward the way they had come in. "Let's take a break."

The jewelry and hair bones hit the sidewalk the instant they were outside. She took Tony's offered jacket, flipping up the hood to block the absurdly bright sun, and wasted no time climbing the single tree in the employee break area. Oak, like the one that held her treehouse.

"I know I'm a hypocrite," she said after a few minutes of silence. "Complaining about being made to look like some cavewoman raised by wild animals or something, and then instantly climbing a tree because I can't deal with the real world anymore."

Tony shrugged from the picnic table. "Not my first client who had a breakdown over creative differences. First one who climbed a tree because of it, but...."

"Raptors," she explained. "They can't get you when you're in a tree. I feel safe here." She saw him mouth the word "raptors," and preempted his question. "Not velociraptors. In real life, those are just little jerks the size of a turkey."

"Then what were they?"

Veronica shrugged. "I'm not a paleontologist. They were big, they wanted to eat me; whether they were utahraptors or deinonychus, I didn't know and I didn't care." She closed her eyes, pulling the jacket around her tighter and running a hand through nearby leaves so the sound would drown out the irritating static of traffic.

"You disappeared when you were a kid," Tony said. "The clothes you were wearing when you came back. . . ."

"There are other people. Towns, even. But by the time I figured that out, I was good at . . . what did you call it the other day, *Land of the Lost*-ing it? I went to town for clothes and supplies, traded plants for the medicine people made from them, but that's it."

A long moment passed without conversation. Peacefully being in the presence of another living soul without fear of making a social faux pas made it almost feel like home. He just *got* her, a same wavelength kind of thing.

"There's other people," Tony said finally, slowly like the words didn't make sense together.

"From all different times," Veronica confirmed. "I don't understand the physics of it. I just miss it."

"Why haven't you told anyone else this? All of the reporters, scientists. You just tell them you went through a portal, and there were dinosaurs on the other side. And you keep bringing up those plants, asking if they still exist, but you never said other people turn them into medicine."

She opened her eyes, looking down at him. "Told you. I feel safe here."

He nodded slowly, his eyes unfocused and his mind clearly elsewhere, before returning to the present situation. "This," he said, pointing to Veronica curled up on her branch, scared and safe, one with nature while the city loomed behind, wearing an oversized flannel jacket with her cavewoman couture. "This, the juxtapositions. This is the photo they should use."

Interviews never got easier, no matter what Tony told her, no matter how many times she answered the same questions over and over.

"Why did I run away? I didn't run away. I was a kid who grew up on stories about magical worlds, and I stepped through the looking glass. I didn't know it would be gone a few minutes later."

"Of course I was hoping my parents would still be around. I know they never gave up hope, and I'm sorry they didn't live long enough to see me come back."

"What's next for me?"

Veronica started to give the response they had practiced so much it had become almost automatic, the one about trying to go back to normal, getting a job and starting a family. The response that she used to think was true, back when she always had one eye on the lookout for a portal home.

She leaned back in the chair, looking past the interviewer at Tony. He stared at her for a moment, silently begging her to follow the approved script, but eventually gave a dismissive wave as if to say, "You're gonna do it anyway, I'm not going to stop you."

"What's next for me," Veronica repeated. "It would be nice, falling in love and settling down, starting a career. But the longer I'm here, the more I realize I just want to go home."

The interviewer nearly choked on her water. "Home? Do you mean back to Massachusetts where you grew up?"

"I didn't grow up in Massachusetts," Veronica said, watching Tony run a hand through his hair in his anxious way. "I lived there as a child, but I grew up in Avalonia. The outskirts of what used to be the kingdom of Camelops. That's home. I just need to find a portal, or figure out how to open one."

"I said the wrong thing," Veronica says, running her hand

through the leaves hanging over the treehouse balcony. It almost drowns out the sound of all the people. The construction vehicles.

Gertie nudges her. Gently, as her head has grown with the rest of her and she doesn't want to knock Veronica out of the tree.

"I didn't know it was the wrong thing. I didn't know mentioning the other people, and the medicine. . . . I didn't know it would lead to this."

The media never really forgot the girl who disappeared without a trace only to come back with stories of a parallel universe full of dinosaurs. As weeks turned to months, however, the initial frenzy of constant interviews became occasional requests for product endorsements and the odd invitation to museum galas.

And through it all, Veronica kept one eye open for the portal home.

It never appeared, and as months threatened to become years, she had to face the distinct possibility that it never would.

"I could be stuck here," she said to Tony, who was becoming less her publicist and more her friend every day.

He nodded, reaching for the tree trunk to steady himself. Not a natural climber, Tony. "Do you think it's time to start making a life here? You know I love you, kid, but if you want to move out of my guestroom, get your own apartment, be independent—"

"I don't want a life here. I don't want . . ." She gestured at his house, his world, him. "I don't want to spend the next ten years of my life forging friendships and family and interests because I'll miss them so much if a portal ever opens up."

She spoke with a certain kind of finality. In her mind, there was no scenario in which she would stay, and it took Tony a few tries to form a response.

"And what if it never does? I don't want you to miss out on a good life because you're holding out for a great one, kid."

He was right. He was absolutely right, and she hated that. Chaos and chance had already given her two portals, two once in a million lifetimes occurrences, and here she was, arrogant enough to assume she would get a third?

An image of herself, old and alone and still sleeping in Tony's guestroom, forced its way into her mind. No family, no scrapbooks full of memories, just a stubborn woman on a borrowed deathbed, surrounded by regrets.

"I made a promise to a friend," Veronica said quietly. "I said I'd be right back."

Tony took her hand. Mostly to keep himself steady as a strong wind shook the tree, she suspected, but he kept holding it afterward. "I'm a friend. Make me a promise."

"What kind of promise?"

"Do something. I'm not asking you to make a huge commitment like buying a house or anything, but just . . . do one thing that it would be pointless to do if you were leaving tomorrow but you would regret not doing if that portal never opens."

They made the announcement over the radio the first time Veronica was behind the wheel after getting her license, and she nearly lost control of the car.

"I heard that wrong," she said. Insisted.

Tony shook his head. "No, you didn't."

She had to pull over, incidentally on the same stretch of highway where she had reappeared, although she didn't realize it. Too many emotions fought for dominance inside her.

She could go back. But would they let her? This couldn't have been done for her benefit. So what did they want with it? And what damage would it cause?

And was this all her fault?

"If I hadn't come back," she said, squeezing the steering wheel so her hands wouldn't shake, "they wouldn't have ever known there was another world next to ours."

"I know."

"They wouldn't have dedicated so much time and money into the research to find it."

Tony sighed. "I know."

"What are they doing over there, why did they want—" Veronica stopped. She looked at Tony, leaning back in his seat with a look of resigned defeat rather than surprise or outrage. "You know. What does that mean, you know? You know someone has been trying to force portals into existence since the day I got back?"

He ran a hand through his hair. "I knew after you told Channel 5 news that there were other people in your world. Some scientist contacted me, wanting to talk to you. Before you said that, they thought you were just some weird temporal anomaly. Guessing as soon as they learned you weren't the only one, they figured there was some replicable science behind it. And if they could replicate it, they could go there."

"The leaves."

"A lot of money in the miracle drug business I guess," Tony confirmed grimly.

Veronica shut off the car and flung herself out of it, heading for the trees beyond the shoulder of the road. She shouldn't resent Tony for not telling her, for trying to do damage control with the scripted answers. She shouldn't, and maybe one day she wouldn't, but that was not today.

"You really think they'll fall for this?" Veronica asked, feigning leaning on Tony for support so she could whisper in his ear.

"Already have. They wouldn't have invited us otherwise." He paused to reconsider. "Not without it being a big press event, anyway."

"Dressing me up in that hideous fur bikini for my reintroduction into the wild," Veronica said with a laugh she had to disguise as a weak cough as they approached yet another security guard at yet another set of locked doors at Electrum Industries.

"I didn't mind the fur bikini," Tony teased once they had been buzzed through. "But trust me. They think you're sick and your migraine plant is some sort of prehistoric cure-all—"

"A panacea from Pangea."

"—so they'll agree to all of our terms if you'll be their guide and help them get their hands on it."

"But when it doesn't do anything more than pain relief?"

"That's a tomorrow problem," he said. "Today, we just have to get you home."

Where the natural portals looked like a gentle glimmering glitch in reality, this one was a gaping wound, held open and prevented from healing by some sort of frame made of glass tubes pulsating with small bursts of electricity. Like those plasma ball things Veronica remembered making her hair stand on end when she touched them at the science museum.

It had to be twenty feet high, and nearly as wide. This time, Veronica didn't need to feign weakness, leaning on Tony for support as her legs threatened to give out.

"Why is it so big?" she asked, dreading the answer. She loved the second *Jurassic Park*, but that didn't mean she wanted to be responsible for recreating the tyrannosaurus rampage in San Diego.

Somehow, the man in charge found a worse answer Veronica had never considered. "So we can bring the trucks in."

"It's beautiful," Tony breathed.

"It was," Veronica corrected.

Even in the more civilized parts of Avalonia, it wasn't industrialized. Some electricity, sure, running water and solar panels and refrigeration, but all in moderation. People who couldn't or wouldn't go home, who had never known a home apart from this world, acknowledging the effect their existence had on the world and creatures around them and trying to minimize it.

Veronica opened and closed her hands helplessly, as if grasping for the memory of her quiet, pristine slice of nature. She couldn't hear the wilderness over the roar of trucks bringing supplies to the construction site, couldn't smell the flowers through the noxious exhaust.

"They can't do this," she said. She turned to the construction foreman. "You can't do this. A visitor center? Really? You find the one untouched piece of land and you just have to touch it, don't you?"

Tony's hand was on her arm, his mouth at her ear. "You're home. Let that be enough for today, we can work on the rest tomorrow."

Reluctantly, she nodded. "But my treehouse better still be there, and my Gertie."

"I don't know what a Gertie is," the foreman said, "but the construction is limited to this area. No treehouses were harmed. Now about that plant...."

In retrospect, Veronica probably shouldn't have done this, but at the time she was too preoccupied with whether it would be funny to screw with someone who probably thought Hexxus was the protagonist of *FernGully*. "Oh, the plant? Yes, I believe it was growing right about..." She pointed at the newly poured concrete foundation. "There."

"I can't fix what's happened," Veronica says. "I can't make that world forget about this one, or stop certain people from wanting to exploit the resources here. Probably can't even close the portal they've opened."

She runs a finger along the wood grain of the balcony. The treehouse was there when she arrived as a child, somebody else's abandoned sanctuary waiting to welcome the next generation of lost little girls.

"Our world has been through a lot of changes," she tells Gertie, giving the sauropod a gentle pat on the nose. "The library in New Hell Creek says it was probably empty at first, just a place where the portals met. Then the animals came through, and the people, and they built towns and domesticated dinosaurs. Fought wars. And none of that could be undone, but the world adapted."

Veronica can't help wondering if this change will be the one that ruins at all, though. Compared to a few people riding a few raptors and cutting down a tree or two, this could be the meteorite that ends everything.

The whole Earth knows about Avalonia. Even if she and Tony succeed, her secret world isn't a secret anymore. This changes everything, for both worlds.

"But we'll be all right. We'll adapt, we'll survive. It's all we can do. Life doesn't know how to give up."

Gertie closes her eyes and snorts again, then looks off to the side at the sound of someone calling out in confusion.

"Veronica? Veronica Moore?"

"How many Veronicas does he think are around here?" Veronica asks Gertie before leaning out over the balcony and whistling. "Over here."

Tony heads in their direction but freezes in place upon seeing the sauropod.

"Tony, meet my friend Gertie. Gertie, this is Tony. Don't step on him."

Tony freezes. "Is that … is that something I have to worry about?"

After considering it for a moment, Veronica shrugs. "I don't know, she wasn't this big last I saw her." She grins at his hesitation. "She's a sweetheart. What's the verdict?"

He gives her a thumbs up, and a wave of relief crashes over her.

The past is the past, what's done is done. They can't change any of it. But they can protect the future, limit the damage and exploitation of this wonderfully weird world by turning the area around the treehouse into a nature preserve.

It isn't much, it isn't enough, but it's a start. Protecting the rest of Avalonia is a tomorrow problem.

"Hey," Veronica says softly to Tony. "You want to come up? We can turn the balcony into a guestroom."

Prehistoric in Pink

Senior prom was the Cretaceous-Paleogene boundary.

Now, you may think it overly dramatic to compare a school dance to the cataclysmic extinction event that killed the dinosaurs, and you would be correct. Claire Baker, like most teenagers, struggled with the concept of geologic timescales, as they measured in millions of years and failed to take into account that this coming Saturday was, in fact, the most important thing that would ever occur in the history of everything.

And she didn't even have a date.

"Just ask him."

Claire looked at her friend incredulously. "Just ask him. Becky, I can't . . ." She made vague but emphatic gestures of helplessness toward the boy in question. "I can't just ask him."

Becky frowned, tearing off a piece of her sandwich and tossing it to the little feathered dinosaur she had been trying and failing to befriend all year. "It's the 2060s, girls can ask out boys."

"Not this girl, not that boy. Why don't you ask him?"

"Can't. Lesbian," Becky teased.

With a groan of frustration, Claire flung herself back from the picnic table, landing on the grass with a satisfying thud.

She stared up at the sky, annoyed that it was so perfectly blue and devoid of any clouds she could pretend looked like her and John. His cloud would have been much more impressive than hers, cumulonimbus probably, drifting confidently in the breeze, while hers was a collection of contrails, polluted and gross and being phased out of the world.

"Because he's from the future," Claire said, interrupting Becky before she could ask. "They've got flying cars—"

"They do not have flying cars," Becky corrected.

"And a post-capitalist society—"

"No, that's *Star Trek*."

"Everything over there is so hyperbolic—"

"I don't think you know what hyperbolic means."

"His world is so different and amazing, what could he possibly want with someone from now?"

"Claire, he is literally from two years in the future, what are you talking about?"

Claire grumbled at the sky. "Just let me pretend that's a valid reason so I don't have to confront my insecurities."

She confronted her insecurities anyway. She couldn't help it, they confronted her first.

When Claire was a kid, her father took her to the circus to see the performing dinosaurs. The audience had to sit far from the rings, "for safety," as the trained triceratops paraded around with streamers on their horns and raptor tamers faced certain death going through routines with a deinonychus pack.

But they weren't actual creatures from Avalonia, they were robotic, and Claire was asked to leave when she pointed that out.

As long as there had been human society, or at least as long as there had been high school, there had been mechanical circuses made of people who found reasons to pretend they were better than others. Gender, race, socioeconomic status . . . nothing that inherently carried any particular morality, but the magic was in the pretending.

Lie with confidence, punish anyone who dares push back, and suddenly you're the dominant species in the ecosystem.

John's family had the connections to visit Avalonia, to relocate two years earlier so his mother could work on the new portal project, and people said that made him important until it became true.

"You know, he's really not that special," Claire lied to Becky and herself. "So he's seen our school mascot in the wild, big deal. I could do better."

"You definitely could."

"He's not even particularly attractive if you actually look at him. He's—"

He was in her field of vision, beaming down at her with that smile brighter than her future and those eyes that were literally, no exaggeration, the most hyperbolic things Claire had ever seen.

"Hey," John said, "would you want to go to the prom with me?"

"Yes."

Becky gave a deep sigh of disappointment.

The Cretaceous-Paleogene boundary marked a drastic change in the status quo. On one side of that thin strip of iridium splattered across the planet by the fateful asteroid, fossils pasted in geological scrapbooks told of a world ruled by terrible lizards, a paradise wiped out in a relative instant that paved the way for mammals to put up parking lots.

Veronica Moore's return and subsequent reveal of Avalonia was another asteroid. The world before humanity developed portal technology would never, could never, exist again. For better or worse, everything had changed.

Which is precisely why Claire needed a prom dress from the 1980s.

Ellen, who owned the travel agency where Claire worked after school, listened carefully to this explanation. She thought for a moment, drawn-on eyebrows furrowed and bright red lips scrunched up in an annoyingly attractive way.

"Nope," she said finally, pushing away from the counter and going back to the brochures she had been putting up. "I'm not following."

Claire grabbed another stack and went with her. "Prom is the last big event of high school. The geologic strata of my life is going to be divided into before prom and after prom, everything will be different, I get to reinvent myself."

"You can reinvent yourself any day, honey," Ellen pointed out. "But I'm picking up what you're putting down and I'll see if I can find you some extra shifts. What kind of dress are you thinking?"

With a giddy smile, Claire flipped through the brochures on the racks until she found the right one. Neon words invited customers to "visit the totally rad 80s," with packages ranging from day trips to parts of Avalonia modeled after the decade (optional meet and greet with minor celebrities available for an additional fee) to actual discreet excursions to 1987 via a stable wormhole.

"This," she said, pointing at a hideous monstrosity of pink taffeta. She wouldn't be able to afford the genuine article, but the re-creations made by Avalonia's craftspeople had a more modern flair that she quite liked. "I want this. I want to be someone who goes to Avalonia, I want to be fancy and cool like John."

Ellen made no attempt to hide her opinion of the dress, but supported Claire nevertheless. "Being fancy and cool is expensive," she said, pointing at the old woman walking in the door. "Go earn a commission."

Claire's sales pitch replayed in her dreams that night, all of her awkwardness and nerves stripped away and replaced with the confidence and charisma she would have on the other side of prom night's iridium boundary.

None of the fumbling to find the right brochure, no "I forget how much that costs, let me ask my manager," just words flowing without effort, charming customers, smiles that made a little sparkle sound.

"And of course, for the discerning traveler who prioritizes the human connection," she said, elegantly moving across the sales floor, "we have meet and greet galas. For one reasonably priced ticket, you can attend a party in fabulous Central Avalonia along with a variety of history's most famous names and faces."

The old woman looked skeptical. "Such as?"

"Lord Byron is a frequent guest," Claire said, and in her dream she felt herself rising up as the light in the store focused around her.

"As is his daughter Ada, the Countess of Lovelace."

She was in the spotlight now, standing on a platform. She didn't know how she felt about this.

"Debate ethics with Aristotle, find out what really happened to Amelia Earhart, do you like Lewis Carroll—"

Faint circus music began growing louder, distracting Claire.

"Lewis Carroll, uh, the pen name of Charles Dodgson? We got Dodgson here, and—"

She turned around, and saw smaller spotlights illuminating the figures as she named them. Somewhere in the distance, she could hear her younger self being asked to leave.

Her father was being hyperbolic. Probably. One of these days, Claire would learn exactly what that meant.

(This was a lie she told herself, but it made her feel better so she didn't mind.)

"But Dad," she argued, trying to sound as mature as the conversation she wanted to have and succeeding in only a marginal amount of whining. "Prom is—"

"I know," he interrupted gently as he set the table for breakfast. "Prom is geology, it's important to you. But you don't need a dress from Avalonia."

Claire frowned and flipped the last pancake onto a plate. "You don't like John."

Her father thought for a moment. "No, not particularly. I like Becky."

Claire murmured something bisexual, and her father grinned.

"But I trust you. I just don't want you going to Avalonia, even to buy a prom dress."

The lights in their minuscule kitchen dimmed as they started to eat. They shared a power grid with the local portal station, and residential areas didn't seem to be anybody's priority.

All the more reason for her father to have a grudge against Avalonian tourism, Claire supposed. But it was just a dress, just a quick visit to another breathtaking world.

What could it hurt?

She nodded, indicating she understood. If he chose to believe she was agreeing, Claire couldn't help that.

Electrum Industries had the audacity to announce that the first demonstration of their new technology would take place the same evening as senior prom.

With a swipe of her hand, Claire dismissed the holographic newsfeed projected from her bracelet and flopped back on what was quickly becoming her own personal patch of dramatic moment grass. "Not to be hyperbolic, but this is literally the worst thing that has ever happened to me."

Becky's eyes lit up. "Hey, you used it correctly this time!"

"Did I?"

Becky nodded, licking a bit of cheese sauce from her thumb. She did look rather hyperbolic when she did that, Claire thought, and blushed.

"Okay, circling back, why is this the worst thing that has happened to you? Because I also don't like it, but I don't think it's for the same reason."

Claire brought up the newsfeed again and pushed it in the general direction of the table before throwing her arms over her face for added visual effect. "People are already protesting."

"As they should," Becky said. She made little enticing noises at the feathered dinosaur who, judging by the annoyed grumble that followed, continued to have no interest in friendship. "Industrialization is ruining Avalonia's ecosystem, I can only imagine the impact on other times when we can freely open portals that lead wherever we want in our timeline."

"But I need to go to Electrum so I can get my dress and they probably won't let anybody in."

She regretted the words instantly, and the silence from Becky was deafening with disappointment.

She had the dream again that night.

One customer after another, listening to Claire extol the virtues of visiting Avalonia as the spotlight grew tighter and her platform grew taller. There was a crowd now, and she didn't know when that happened.

She gave her sales pitch, sounding more and more like a circus ringleader with every historical figure that appeared in spotlights. The stylized E of the Electrum Industries logo emblazoned itself across her chest as her sponsor.

There was another figure in the darkness, the lights around her dimming too much to see her properly. Claire recognized the silhouette and waited for her younger self to point out that it was all fake, but her younger self had been asked to leave a while ago.

The final spotlight snapped on, painfully bright, revealing herself in the pink dress, staring blankly at the crowd.

"I don't want to be a mechanical dinosaur."

Ellen chuckled. "I do love your non sequiturs."

Claire almost smiled. "Fake," she elaborated. "Trying to be something I'm not just to impress people. Lying."

It was the morning of the senior prom, the morning before the asteroid that would officially close the chapter of childhood and let her start a new, adult life on a sparkling layer of iridium.

And she had picked up a shift at Ellen's purely to have an excuse not to be one of those people on the video feeds walking through the protests surrounding Electrum. Did she need a dress, that dress, so badly?

Part of her said yes. She hoped that part would go extinct after prom.

Claire fiddled with the edge of a pamphlet, tearing it with her fingernails as she stared through the holographic news. "I was thinking about going to get the dress and then returning it after so Dad wouldn't find out I went to Avalonia."

Ellen was silent for a moment. "Your father isn't trying to keep you away from Avalonia," she said quietly. "And his reasons go beyond raising you to share his values."

Claire looked up at her, frowning. "He's very clearly trying to keep me away from Avalonia."

"No, he's trying to keep you away from Electrum Industries tonight. There's a difference." Ellen let that sink in before switching effortlessly back to chatty boss/aunt figure mode. "You don't need an extinction event to reinvent yourself. Every day, every moment, you can declare a new geological era and decide not to be a mechanical dinosaur anymore."

Senior prom was the Cretaceous-Paleogene boundary.

That night marked a new era for Earth, for Avalonia, but most importantly for Claire and Becky. Nothing would ever be the same, no going back.

Electrum Industries briefly became the sole proprietor of time travel technology, making it possible for people to open portals leading directly to any point in the timeline they desired. "Briefly" being the operative word.

The explosion destroyed the only completed portal, granting the timeline a few weeks' reprieve from the corrupting intrusion and industrialization Avalonia had suffered. They would finish the second, but not tonight.

In the morning, Claire would find Ellen's travel agency closed until further notice, no explanation or forwarding address, just a note that said, "Good luck, kid." Claire would choose to believe Ellen escaped to Avalonia and wasn't among the victims she would eventually start to think of as martyrs.

She would find police questioning her father about his involvement, but he would never admit anything. One day, she would realize he was trying to keep her safe, not just from the investigation but from a world controlled by Electrum. One day, but not tonight.

In Avalonia—

Well, that is a story that would soon tell itself. But not tonight.

Tonight, Claire and Becky turned off their electronics and spent livious hours dancing in the grass outside school. They wore ordinary dresses that became special in the moonlight, they acted like children, like fools, like however they wanted to start adulthood.

Tonight, they realized the feathered dinosaur Becky wanted to befriend didn't move as smoothly or naturally as the ones who perched in the branches, a chirping chorus gladly catching bits of thrown food. Everything was a mechanical circus, even the school's surveillance system.

Tonight, Claire and Becky felt real. Genuine and honest and full of possibilities, nothing before or after this moment mattered. They stopped thinking about whether they should, only if they could.

Their first kiss sparkled like iridium.

Iguanodon Quixote

Our lawyer paces, worrying his hand over his chin and mouthing occasionally to himself before dismissing the thought with a shake of his head. Nice man, Martin. We're supposed to hate lawyers, supposed to think of them as soulless monsters on par with used car salesmen. But this one's cool.

(And as the granddaughter of a used car salesman, I try to look past what society tells us about who the monsters are.)

I share a hopeless look with my best friend. We were resigned to our fate before it happened, only Martin is still trying to get us out of here.

"The only one we've got on our side is the bloodsucking lawyer," I whisper, and Mel gives me a halfhearted nudge about the *Jurassic Park* reference.

"We're guilty," she reminds Martin.

"Well. Yes. Therein lies the problem of defending you in court." He gestures at the bookshelves lining his office, filled with a mismatch of legal tomes from a variety of times and places. "Avalonian law is chaotic, borrows ideas from colonial America, ancient Greece, feudal Japan, twenty-second-century Palestine . . . but the one thing they all have in common is that they want the guilty parties to lose."

"Any of them let you win if you convince the jury you did the right thing?" I joke. At least, I think I'm joking.

Martin laughs but there's no humor on his face. "If you stole bread to feed your family, absolutely. Not for terrorism."

"Do we have anything to lose by trying?"

They both look at me. I don't think I'm joking.

"Look at how popular opinion changes, though," I insist. "Iguanodon for example. People used to think dinosaurs were monsters—"

"People died," Mel says, as if I don't see their faces every time I close my eyes. "We don't get to walk away from this, no matter how justified it is in the grand scheme."

Though he stops pacing in front of us, Martin still shifts his weight anxiously. "She's right. I support the cause, Kayla, you know I do, but it took over one hundred years for popular opinion about iguanodon to evolve from monster to living, breathing animal. We don't have that long."

I shouldn't be this afraid. We were always meant to be martyrs.

"Please. Let me try. I'll spare no expense."

This nudge from Mel has actual emotion behind it. "You can't *Jurassic Park* reference your way out of everything."

"The voice you are now hearing is Richard Kiley."

Mel buries her face in her hands and mutters something that sounds like a swear. Multiple, actually.

"Trust me," I whisper, letting the judge and jury be moved by the deep baritone singer.

"That's the problem," she says. "I do trust you."

From the other side of me, our lawyer leans in and says, "I don't trust you. But I'm hopeful."

Yeah. That's fair.

The courtroom, styled more or less like something from *Law and Order* (specifically the one with Jeff Goldblum), has surprisingly good acoustics that give an impressive echo effect to the song playing from Martin's phone. For possibly the first time in my life, I sit quietly and just listen.

The flag of Avalonia hangs above the judge. Tricolor stripes of blue, white, and red provide the background for a maroon and gold archaeopteryx flying free from broken chains.

My flag. My home. My people and my land and my reason for everything.

I cross my fingers, kiss them for luck, and mouth the words to

"The Impossible Dream" like it's our national anthem. Mel does the same, although I'm not sure she knows the words.

The song fades, and now it's all me. I squeeze Mel's hand, blink away my tears, and stand.

"*Man of La Mancha*," I say. I wish my voice sounded more confident. "Based on *Don Quixote*, about a foolish old man fighting windmills because they might be giants to win the heart of a girl who doesn't know he exists." I point at the phone. "Richard Kiley was the first to play the main character, Miguel Cervantes, but the musical goes on even after his death. Same story, different stars."

The judge already looks annoyed. That is . . . not ideal. I need a different story, something that will resonate with people at the DNA level. Something eternal, timeless, the kind of story we invented language to tell and will be telling with our last breaths.

"Alice," I say, and I wonder if I should go out and pace in front of the bench for dramatic effect. "We all know about Alice, the little girl who became the very first human being to set foot in what we now call Avalonia. Can you imagine her on that beach, eating her roast beef sandwich, completely unaware of the prehistoric wonders just on the other side of reality?"

A couple of the jurors frown and mumble to each other. So maybe I'm changing the details, a story doesn't need to be accurate to be true. It just needs to be a good story properly told.

"What are you doing?" Martin whispers at the same time I hear Mel groan, "Oh no."

"She wandered away from her parents," I continue, clasping my hands in front of me so people don't see them shake, "only realizing she had left her world behind when she saw the allosaurus and called out, 'Mommy, Daddy, I found something!'"

Mel kicks my leg, hard. "Please tell me you are not making this *Jurassic Park* right now."

"I promise I'm not." Technically, this is *The Lost World: Jurassic Park*. Totally different movie.

Look, maybe I'm autistic and a little obsessed, maybe I'm just really in love with Jeff Goldblum, but *Jurassic Park* is the ultimate story of humanity. It's Prometheus, it's *Frankenstein*, it's the bisexual awakening we all needed that taught us about hubris and the importance of protecting the ecosystem for our children.

But more importantly, it's the only thing I can think of at the moment.

Maybe I'm too idealistic, but there's something uniquely heartbreaking and radicalizing about watching people step into a sprawling land of prehistoric wonder humanity was never meant to see . . . and throwing cigarette butts on the ground.

"Please," I said as politely as I could manage to the tour group who clearly had no interest in showing a little respect. "Hold onto your butts and candy wrappers until we get back to the visitor center and find some garbage cans."

The tourists grumbled but didn't complain openly until the first raindrops began to fall. The mother threatened the sky to mind its own business and asked me if they would get their money back if the trip got ruined.

"Ruined?" I asked, handing out yellow rain slickers and trying to sound chipper. "If we go down to the creek, this might actually give us a rare opportunity to see some beelzebufo coming up out of the water—"

I was informed this was not as exciting as I thought, by people who already seemed bored with the parasaurolophus choir singing in the distance.

Avalonia was my home. I loved it, loved my community, wouldn't give it up for anything. But sometimes I thought humanity being there was a mistake.

That's when I met him. Handsome black man in his 40s, polite enough but clearly tired of dealing with people who irritated him.

Opposing counsel interrupts my story. "Objection! The defendant is describing Samuel L. Jackson from *Jurassic Park*."

Mel and Martin mutter "Oh god" on either side of me.

The judge looks at me, raises an eyebrow. "Ms. Richards?"

"I am most certainly not describing Samuel L. Jackson from *Jurassic Park*, Your Honor." It's the truth. I'm not.

I was, but I just decided I'm not anymore.

When the judge nods, I continue, "He asked me to join a team he was putting together. . . ."

Realizing I am describing Samuel L. Jackson from *The Avengers*, Martin touches my arm. "Don't commit perjury in the service of a good story," he says under his breath. "Skip ahead before you say he has an eyepatch."

Older folks in Avalonia will tell you we used to coexist with nature, that we respected the ecosystem that was here before us, limiting our impact as much as possible while carving out little echoes of civilization in a world where we were welcome if not strictly invited.

Electrum Industries propaganda will tell you we used to live like savages. They will tell you we suffered with sunny side up eggs from oviraptors you knew the name of, that the most important meal of the day is artificially colored breakfast cereal you saw advertised on television.

They will tell you we aren't civilized until we eradicate the natural world, and you will believe them. They tell a good story, but they tell it for the wrong reasons.

I wanted to believe them. Even though I mourned the Avalonia that had already been dying in my half-remembered childhood, I wanted to fool myself into believing there were people making our world better.

That hope went extinct the instant the five of us set foot in Electrum headquarters.

Everything was fake. The plants, the people, the lighting. They murdered god and Mother Nature and laughed along to elevator music at the funeral.

Everything was as fake as our credentials and undercover identities.

Opposing counsel is going to object again, I can see it on his face. Relevancy, that's what he'll say, and the judge will ask me to get to the point and skip all the backstory.

But the backstory is the point. It's the only point. I can't defend what we did, I can only try to convince them it was the right thing.

"You know the names and faces of the people who died there," I say, wishing we were in a theater setting and I could show a presentation. "They were real people, not autoerotics—"

"Automatons," Mel corrects.

"—with hopes and impossible dreams of their own. You vilify us for getting them killed, and rightly so."

Martin's chair squeaks as he sits up in alarm. "Kayla," he cautions.

"But what about the other victims?" I challenge, and there are countless examples I could give but I focus on the reasons our team signed up. "What about Jophrey's brother, killed by the mesonychid poached from the wilds of Avalonia and brought to Earth under the lie that it was domesticated and safe to keep as a pet?"

I need sweeping music. Mouthing my request to Martin, I slide his phone toward him as I continue.

"What about the Hildebrand Farm, sustainably feeding families in Avalonia for three generations only to go out of business almost overnight because who can compete with a bright and shiny supermarket?"

The first notes of John Williams and his orchestra start to play, and Mel just shakes her head. It's my fault she's here. I don't know if I can fix that, I don't know if I can get her out, but I can at least try to save our home.

"What about Udesky, struggling to survive after a workplace accident because he lived in a time without disability benefits and the company he worked for decided this was the one time they wanted to respect the timeline?" I look around expectantly. "Do you care about the victims of Electrum? Do you know our names and faces? Have you seen the devastation they brought to our world, our home? The devastation they want to bring to the entire timeline back on Earth?"

I have to put my hand on the table to steady myself, remembering to breathe while I blink away the tears forming in my eyes.

"Do you care," I implore as the music rises, "that we are about to see dinosaurs go extinct again and we are doing nothing to stop it?"

Before anyone can object, before I can ruin the moment by rambling more, Martin calls a brief recess so he can take a bio break.

"See?" I whisper to Mel as the lawyer goes to the bathroom. "I'm not the only one who can make *Jurassic Park* references."

She gives me a long-suffering look, just utter, soul-deep exhaustion and hopelessness. Not at me, at least not entirely, but I know my nonsense isn't helping.

None of this was my plan. I can't take credit as the mastermind terrorist or blame as the conniving savior. But I'm the one who brought Mel in. She's on trial right now because we needed a historian on the team and like a fool, I said, "I know a historian."

I don't care what happens to me or my reputation. Execute me as a cautionary tale, slander my name and turn me into a cartoon villain in the popular culture of future generations.

All that matters is that my best friend is still my best friend at the end of the day, that she doesn't regret having known me.

I nudge her foot with mine. "I think sometimes I get too preoccupied with whether I could make *Jurassic Park* references, and I don't stop to think if I should."

She rolls her eyes, but there's a smile. Little one, but it's there.

The five of us started working at Electrum about a month before they opened the portal in time. The three guys—we didn't get to know them as well as I would have liked—in security, engineering, and reception. Mel was in research and record keeping, ostensibly finding ways to limit the butterfly effect, though I doubted anyone at the company cared about the timeline more than their bottom line.

And then there was me, the tour guide, doing what I do best: talking at length to people who wished I had stopped talking about five minutes ago. Sometimes selling the idea of Avalonia to investors looking for new franchise locations, sometimes taking them on unnecessary circuits of the building, stalling them until the bureaucrats secured a better estimate with their competitors.

I was amazing at stalling.

Now, I don't claim to understand the science that let them open stable doorways to any point in time that they liked. I tried to understand, but my brain isn't built for that kind of physics. I cannot exaggerate how much I was there just to stall for time.

It used the same technology that let them open portals to Avalonia, at any rate, and when they had more than one up and running, they would be able to control all of them with a single switch. "For safety reasons," I would say during my tours, "an emergency shutdown in case anything goes wrong."

Not that anything would go wrong. No, they spared no expense to ensure they were in complete control.

But that kind of control simply isn't possible. Time will not be contained, time breaks free, time—

"Objection!"

Finally.

"Defense is merely going over the facts that have already been covered while making references to a movie none of us care about."

Mel puts her hand on my arm as if to stop me from launching myself at opposing counsel at the same time Martin warily whispers, "Kayla...."

"I'm fine," I promise them. And in fact, I'm better than fine. Prosecution just gave me the perfect setup for my big reveal.

The judge glares down at me. "Perhaps defense would like her legal representation to finish?"

"No, I'm good," I assure him. "Can I step out here, do a little dramatic pacing?"

Nobody tries to stop me, so I take that as a yes.

"We are guilty. We have never denied that, and you all decided it before the trial even began. There is nothing I can say to change your minds."

Martin and Mel do not return my thumbs up.

"I hope some of what I say here could change your hearts, make you understand why we did what we did. But if you want some facts you don't already have? I've got one for you, a real fun one actually."

I pause here, wishing I had thought to start the music again for extra drama.

"There was a sixth person on our team that we've never mentioned in any of our statements."

There's a murmur among the jury. I feel like grinning. I feel like throwing up.

"When the five of us were destroying the time portal, Ellen was setting up the dominoes and they are falling as we speak, people." With my hands squeezed into fists so nobody can see them shaking, I turn and address everyone from Electrum who had testified throughout the day. "CEO. Chief of security. Head of research and development. You . . . honestly I don't remember who you are, but you were important. You are all important. And you're here, all of you, away from the company."

For the first time today, Mel looks hopeful. Not for me, not for her, but for Avalonia.

I didn't tell Martin the entire plan. Plausible deniability and all that. But I can see him connecting the dots, figuring out what I'm up to, and he's grinning.

"You're here, and your company is in the hands of a surprising number of people who believe in our cause more than they believe in yours. We made sure they were safe that night, Ellen made sure, and then she made sure some of us survived to have a trial that would draw all of you away from Electrum."

Prosecution wants to object. Hell, the judge looks like he wants to object. But they all just sit in silence, baffled and scrambling to understand what's going on.

"I'm not trying to defend our actions, I never have been, I've just been stalling for time," I tell them, laughing and crying all at once. "We have the emergency cutoff switch, and we can control more than just the time portals."

Now they object. Everyone, even the jury, the courtroom growing louder and louder as people demand . . . well, to be honest I'm not sure what they are demanding. I don't think they do, either.

"There will be no more stable portals to Avalonia!" I have to shout to be heard. It feels good to shout this. "There will be no more portals at all!"

That one may be an exaggeration. Ellen is working on it, she thinks she can prevent even the natural ones from opening.

"We can't fix the damage we have done, but we can decide to close the wounds!"

There is more I could say, but nobody is listening to me anymore. At least not right now. Maybe someday.

I don't know what happens next. With us, with Avalonia. I only know that when I look over at Mel, she's beaming through her tears and mouthing two words.

"Clever girl."

Allosaurus Through the Looking Glass

'Twas not brillig the evening I stepped into the wormhole.

I knew what that word meant now. Maybe not in *Jabberwocky*, not the original meaning Lewis Carroll intended, if he even had a meaning in mind when he wrote that beautiful nonsense.

I met him once, and Alice twice (the first time when she was young, the second when she was old and said it was the third, both when I was in my twenties). Our conversations wandered a winding path through math and logic and fantasy but never arrived at the meaning of brillig.

Maybe it meant something different for everyone. For me, it was a more acute version of nostalgia, the realization that you would one day look back with bittersweet, heartbreaking aching for the current moment. The awareness that right now would all too soon become way back when, the sepia filter flashbacks with details slowly slipping away until they become a vague notion of something beautiful you've lost forever.

And even knowing this in the moment, even promising yourself to cherish and remember every moment, every day in that perfect time and space that you will cry yourself to sleep over having lost one day, even that knowledge can't do anything to stop it from happening.

That is my definition of brillig, and I felt it for my childhood that morning I chased the not-quite-rabbit into the portal, and I felt it for the world on the other side that would one day become known as Avalonia.

'Twasn't brillig anymore in Avalonia. What could have, should have, been an untouched pocket of wilderness somewhere between universes had been spoiled, trampled on, and so was the world I grew up believing 'twas brillig. (And perhaps 'twasn't grammatically correct, using 'twas in that sentence, but stories don't need to be perfect, or even true, for them to matter.)

It couldn't be fixed, it was far too late for that, but there were some people taking a radical approach to the issue. Permanently severing the connection between Earth and Avalonia, destroying the ability to open portals on command and only letting the natural ones pop up now and then, the way it used to be when everything 'twas brillig.

I needed to know who they were, needed to know their stories before they slipped away in a sepia filter flashback.

So on the day they were set to close off the worlds from each other, I made one last trip to Avalonia.

I knew the importance of stories, how reality became fantasy became reality as the tales we told took on lives of their own. I was a story myself. Rather, Alice was a story.

Not the fictional Alice of Lewis Carroll fame, and not the Alice I met as a little girl and an old lady and a third time yet to come. The Alice I was as a child, the first person to set foot in Avalonia.

My name isn't Alice. My name isn't important.

What's important is the story, the mythology that evolved around the idea of the first human being who saw beauty and curiosity where others would have seen a monster, and had the courage to face her challenges instead of running from them. Almost none of it really happened, and at some point a couple threads of Wonderland got woven in, but that's what we do, people. We make things important, and we borrow the familiar to make something recognizable but entirely new at the same time.

And so I was Alice, my story lovingly shaped by the erosion of time and culture until it wasn't mine anymore. It belonged to everyone.

My world could do with some stories like that, I decided. New heroes, new cautionary tales.

"I thought it would be nice to start with the truth about the end," I explained to the attorney politely hurrying me down the hall. "Straight from the mouth of the martyrs."

Martin gave a dry chuckle. "You are assuming Kayla's testimony is the truth."

We stopped so someone scrambling to carry too many files could pass. The martyrs have been vilified, but they understood the impact of cutting off travel between these worlds, and gave us time for paperwork and heavy decisions that would lead to more paperwork. I wondered how many people were listening to the seconds tick away, waiting until the last possible to decide which world they would call home.

"You think she lied?"

"Honestly, no," he said, bringing me into the storage room where I could read the court transcript. "But if your plan is to take the truth and let it evolve into folklore, you can take the rest of the night off because she already did it."

I didn't mind that. It was her truth, told for a reason, and Earth deserved to hear it.

Kayla Richards came alive through her words, through descriptions of her movement in the courtroom. Her passion and dedication to her world broke my heart and mended it again. Subconsciously, I crossed my fingers and kissed them for luck when I read she had done the same.

"You're a historian?" Martin asked, and I made a vague gesture with my hand as it was more of a hobby. "Do you know why we do that? Kissing our fingers like that?"

I shook my head, and smiled when Kayla mentioned Alice in the transcript. "I know it started with a girl from Vermont who was here in the early days, but I haven't studied that part of Earth history enough to know the significance or where it came from."

"Lindy."

"That sounds right." I pointed at something near the end of Kayla's testimony. "Who's this person she's talking about? Who is Ellen?"

Who is Ellen? The question was simple enough; the answer is anything but.

That court transcript was the only time somebody named Ellen was mentioned in connection with the Electrum Industries incident. That is my preferred term for it. Incident. "Terrorist attack" is absolutely accurate, there's no denying that, but those words put our brains on the defensive, making it difficult to see the gray area between black and white morality. And "heist" may also be accurate, but minimizes the tragic loss of life. "Incident" felt right to me.

At no point before or after Kayla Richards gave that speech had anyone even hinted at another member of the team. She and Mel refused to answer any questions about this mysterious woman, like they were protecting her.

I was foolish enough to believe they would talk to me, so I joined the gaggle of reporters and protesters Mel had gathered. She stood on the balcony of an old treehouse, a tiny scrap of nature in the middle of a city square, drawing everybody's attention for one last press release before Kayla, somewhere, turned off the portals forever.

Her head rested in her hand, her eyes seemed glazed over as she gave short answers made of meaningless sound bites. And then she saw me.

Everything about her posture changed. She straightened, alert, and gave a small smile that would have been a grin if she let it.

Curiouser and curiouser.

I raised my hand. "I have a question about—"

"Ellen," the girl interrupted, and I just nodded. She started to say something, then stopped herself and disappeared into the treehouse.

A moment later, ignoring the boisterous crowd, she walked up to me, hugged me the way strangers don't, and whispered a time and place in my ear.

"What's that?" I whispered back, although the coordinates gave me a pretty good guess.

The people around us prevented Mel from saying all she wanted to, and she hesitated, as if trying to phrase something covertly. "It's where Ellen's story began."

Several years before the incident, folks struggled to make a living in the shadow of Electrum Industries. It was a new world, shared by frightening, monstrous creatures humanity was never meant to deal with. And those creatures, scientific name Executivus assholedon, brought prehistoric animals to the modern world.

They commercialized time travel, industrialized it, all while making it nearly impossible for people to live as they had for decades, centuries even.

Like a damn Billy Joel song, but with dinosaurs.

I tried not to step on butterflies as I made my way through the town, as if that mattered anymore in a world with thylacine joeys in the window of the pet store. Electrum probably collected all the dead butterfly wings, turned them into confetti. Still, I didn't want to have any direct impact on the timeline if I could help it.

Those of you who have figured out the plot twist are probably laughing at me right now.

I did not find Ellen at the coordinates where her story was supposed to begin.

I found people living in a powder keg, waiting for the spark. I found peaceful protest desperately longing to be a revolution. I found a travel agency looking for an assistant manager, but I did not find Ellen.

Instead, I found the Ellen-shaped space in her story. Folklore waiting to be told, waiting for some ordinary someone that history could twist into a hero.

For the second time in my life, I became that person.

By the end of my second year, 'twas brillig being Ellen. I didn't mean to make connections, didn't mean to step on butterflies, but it's difficult to start a revolution without connections.

I did my best not to care about them, but my own personal Cretaceous-Paleogene boundary, as my dear employee Claire would put it, rapidly approached and I felt the premature heartache of her laugh becoming a vague memory.

She was a good kid. Maybe it was selfish of me, but I couldn't give her father an important role in my plan. I couldn't risk him being one of the butterflies crushed under my bright red heels.

She was a bit awkward, but gave a good sales pitch, I thought proudly one day near the end of knowing her, coming out from the back room while she extolled the virtues of meet and greet galas. The customer, an older woman with kind eyes, chuckled a bit at Claire's mention of Lewis Carroll.

Recognition sparked. I handed Claire a broom. "I got this, honey. Can you go clean up in the alley? Damn overgrown knife pigeons got into the garbage again."

The customer smiled at me. "Alice."

"Alice." I put my hand over hers and shook my head, laughing. "There is so much I can't tell you."

"I'll figure it out," she promised with a wink, "and then not tell you."

"Deal." We sat in a silence that 'twas brillig until I remembered to be Ellen again. "Did Claire sell you on a travel package?"

The other Alice, the inspiration for the *Wonderland* books, began telling me about her recent travels through the timeline, life imitating art as she explored curious places and curiouser times. But now she wanted to see the wonders of Avalonia, and I froze.

She couldn't be there when my metaphorical asteroid hit, she couldn't get trapped on that side of her looking glass. She had to come back, I had already met her for my second and her third time.

If everything went according to plan, if everything went as it already had gone, there would be an opportunity for people to return home before travel between worlds was permanently cut off. But that was before my butterflies.

"Dear?" Alice prompted softly.

I chose my words very carefully. "Sometimes I wonder if I'm playing a part or if I'm the playwright."

She thought for a moment. My store's speaker system switched to a Psychedelic Furs song, one of several thousand on my playlist of human history.

Finally, Alice said, "People have been asking that very question for as long as we've been people. Tell me, how does time travel make the answer any different? You do what you must, and you remember to be mindful of tomorrow, and all the tomorrows you won't live to see, then you kiss your crossed fingers and hope for the best."

Nodding, I took a shaky breath. "Don't stay long."

She gave me a smile. "Step on all the right butterflies."

Ellen's story ended just after the trial, with the successful reverse engineering of the portal technology and the development of a way to prevent even the majority of natural portals from opening.

It was more than just me; Kayla, in her words borrowed from a movie, spared no expense bringing the greatest minds of history in on the project and we had invaluable stacks upon stacks of data compiled in the early days of humanity settling in Avalonia, detailing how the portals worked before people interfered. But Ellen got the credit, because sometimes a faceless figurehead makes the best folk hero.

Yes, Ellen's story ended, but there were more stories to be told before we closed the book on Avalonia. I didn't mean for them to be told through me, it just happened like that.

I built the treehouse in the old oak Mel had spoken from, the one bit of forest no one had the heart to pave over even before progress was stopped and the remaining land became a protected nature preserve. At first, I resisted being the one to build it, resisted being anything more than a spectator. But the story finds a way. Whether through fate or temporal paradox, the story will be told.

And so I played my part as I moved back through Avalonia's history. I played the orderly Bev, I smuggled prophecies out of Camelops, I nearly died reuniting a mother with the greatest treasure of all. I even stole a helicopter once, if you can believe that.

I was there, for more stories than even I can remember. Just bit parts, of course. Nobody you could accuse of being famous.

Well . . . for the most part.

If all of my other roles weren't so faceless, if they had become renowned as more than the building blocks of mythology, someone may have noticed they all shared a striking similarity with Aldith, the last queen of Camelops.

I knew every detail of her story, how she and D.B. Cooper schemed to take over and then be overthrown, it had already been told time and time again. I merely had to follow the trail of butter-fly wings I left for myself.

'Twas brillig, being Aldith. I was barely thirty when I became Ellen, aged a decade or so as I moved in reverse along the timeline, but never more than a few years at a time. Aldith and I grew old together, at first by necessity of the long con and then simply be-cause she felt right, even after the kingdom fell and we fled in joyful disgrace to live out the rest of our lives in a little house surrounded by dinosaurs.

I wouldn't say I fell in love with D.B. The occasional romantic spark, but for the most part we simply fell deeply and desperately in familiarity and comfort with each other. He knew my real name and I knew his, but we didn't let that come between us. He was D.B. and I was Allie, and we didn't need to be anyone else.

"What is that, anyway?" he asked as we sat on our porch one evening, listening to a parasaurolophus choir serenading the first wisps of a pink sunset.

I frowned. "This?" I repeated my gesture, crossing my fingers and kissing them. "It's for luck, you know that. There's a treehouse in the future, I was just suddenly hoping it's the tree I found you in."

"Romantic," he pretended to grumble. "No, I mean why. No-body did that in Camelops, except you, that's a New Hell Creek thing."

"It's an Avalonian thing in the future," I corrected, allowing my-self a bit of pride for our part in ending the division. "Lindy Roman used to do it, she was there at the beginning of New Hell Creek. Camelops didn't have her, they had her ex-boyfriend instead."

"But you don't know where she got it?"

I shook my head, but the evening 'twas brillig, so unbelievably brillig. I didn't know, not really, not in any provable, concrete way.

But it was me. I knew it was me, the same way I suddenly knew this quiet life wasn't my epilogue but rather one last emotional flashback in the making.

I listened to the dinosaurs. I inhaled the smell of a forest lost to time. I looked at D.B., and I kissed my crossed fingers, hoping his smile would be the last detail to fade from my memory.

Avalonia 'twas brillig the day they shut down the portals between worlds. For all its problems, for all the damage industrialization and hubris and human interference had caused, this once-untouched paradise still took my breath away.

I didn't want to leave. I truly didn't.

But there's something to be said for the power of a good story properly told, and Avalonia had no shortage of those. I only hoped my chosen destination in the timeline was early enough that Earth could learn from them.

An allosaurus vocalized in the distance. I crossed my fingers and kissed them as the portal closed behind me. I was the first person to set foot in Avalonia, and I was the last to leave.

And as for Earth? 'Twas brillig.

Author's Note

This book has lived in my heart for years.

A therapist suggested I try meditation for my anxiety in 2017. I lasted less than a minute before the image of raptors chasing a steam train popped into my head and demanded a story, and I have not tried to meditate since.

Over the next few years, I wrote a couple stories that weren't explicitly connected but could conceivably take place in the same world if you squinted. I jokingly referred to them as the Jennifer Lee Rossman Cinematic Universe, and dreamed about someday turning them into something more.

But like the DNA sequences in *Jurassic Park*, my plan had gaps. I didn't know where to begin, I didn't know what story I wanted to tell, I didn't know how to put together a book. Luckily, I've got some awesome people who helped me fill those gaps, and they spared no expense helping Avalonia find a way.

So here's to my metaphorical frog DNA:

Mike Phillips, who approached me with the idea of publishing a collection with From Beyond Press, and enthusiastically supported the idea of interconnected stories set in the same world. You have been awesome every step of the way.

Thea Oatman, the very talented cover artist. I may have started crying when I saw the first sketches, that was when it really started feeling real.

Adie, my Internet sister and fellow future ex-Mrs. Malcolm. You encourage this kind of nonsense and I love you for that.

Jace, who took my natural autistic tendency to notice and obsess over details and helped that evolve into a greater awareness of symbolism. I'm a better storyteller because I know you.

Mike, my partner and natural source of lysine, second only to Robert Picardo in my heart. Ha ha, you're attracted to me.

All of my friends and people from the writing world, too many to name but you are all very dear to me.

Everyone involved in making *Jurassic Park*, the movie that made me who I am.

And you, wonderful reader. Thank you for letting me take you on this tour of Avalonia.

About the Author

Jennifer Lee Rossman (they/them) is a queer, disabled, and autistic author and editor from the land of carousels and Rod Serling. They were too preoccupied with whether they could include a *Jurassic Park* reference in this bio, and didn't stop to think if they should. Find more of their work on their website jenniferleerossman.blogspot.com and follow them on Twitter @JenLRossman

Concept sketch by Thea Oatman

www.ingramcontent.com/pod-product-compliance
Lightning Source LLC
Chambersburg PA
CBHW010737100726
47899CB00009B/3089